"If I want to work for your mother, I will!"

Stacy's words came out angrily.

"No you won't. I don't want you around her," Sloan said simply, as though this was a good reason.

"I don't care what you want," she cried, wondering why his dislike for her hurt so much.

"Do you realize," Sloan said softly, "that I could make you change your mind, if I really wanted to? I've held you in my arms. I can feel you react. You aren't exactly frigid, Stacy Weldon, though I don't think you've had much experience."

Her heart beat and her cheeks burned, and her eyes were glued to the broad, rugged strength of his dark chest. "What does that prove?" she whispered.

"That you might be quite willing to do as I ask, if I stayed with you until daylight."

Kiss of
a Tyrant

by

MARGARET PARGETER

Harlequin Books

TORONTO • LONDON • LOS ANGELES • AMSTERDAM
SYDNEY • HAMBURG • PARIS • STOCKHOLM • ATHENS • TOKYO

Original hardcover edition published in 1980
by Mills & Boon Limited

ISBN 0-373-02375-8

Harlequin edition published December 1980

CHAPTER ONE

STACY WELDON rose with a sigh of resignation from her seat by the kitchen stove, speaking to her sister sharply. 'It's all right, June. For goodness' sake stop worrying! I'll go and answer the door. You can feel free to carry on with what you're doing.'

She knew she must sound truculent and she didn't mean to, just as for all she hugged the kitchen stove she didn't really feel the cold. The trouble was she didn't really feel anything these days; the shock which had partly numbed her ever since she had been unfairly dismissed from the large department store where she had worked was still with her. Of that and Basil Bradley, the man responsible, she tried to think as little as possible.

'I'm sorry, June, I'm on my way.' She made an effort to speak more patiently as the doorbell rang again and June, rubbing a floury finger over her nose, stared at her anxiously.

Pausing only to run a comb carelessly through her long silky hair, Stacy walked steadily towards the front door, which was usually kept closed at this time of year. Opening it, she found two people standing on the doorstep. Looking at them without any real interest, she saw a slim, middle-aged woman of around sixty and a much younger man. He was tall with wide shoulders and a lean, hard body, and she thought he might be the woman's son. She wouldn't like to have taken a bet on it, but there did seem to be some slight resemblance.

Because the man appeared the much more dominant personality, it was to him that Stacy turned enquiringly, noting how his eyes seemed to flicker as he met her cool

5

stare. It came to her suddenly that he was not used to being studied with such marked indifference as she displayed. Not by anyone!

'Good morning,' she said slowly, forgetting it was already afternoon.

Neither acknowledged her obviously reluctant greeting immediately, although the woman frowned. After a slight pause the man said curtly, 'This is the Thorn Farm guesthouse, I take it?'

'Yes, that's right.' Stacy didn't feel so much as one small stirring of curiosity. What she did feel, as the man's appraising eyes flicked over her, was too vague to put a name to.

The woman put in quickly, as if sensing her companion's impatience, 'We wished to enquire about accommodation.'

'Then you'd better come in,' Stacy suggested, as though it mattered little to her whether they did or not. She noticed the man's mouth tighten, as if he restrained himself with difficulty from turning and walking away. Let him think what he liked, she thought irritably, she wasn't answerable to him or any man – not now. She stared back at him defiantly.

They were halfway across the hall before she remembered it was not her own livelihood she might be jeopardising but her mother's, if she antagonised two prospective guests. And, if her own image didn't matter any more, she owed her mother too much to repay her like this.

Guiding them into the small office, which served as a reception desk as well as everything else, she managed a pleasant smile while asking politely, 'I suppose you are looking for rooms?'

'We could be,' said the man, uncompromisingly.

Stacy's small but haughty chin lifted at least two inches in unconscious reaction before she checked. Drawing a self-admonitory breath, she tried to explain. 'My mother, Mrs Weldon, usually sees to this sort of thing, but I'm afraid she's out, but if you could tell me exactly what you want, and for how long, I might be able to help you.'

'Indeed?' the man murmured drily, as if surprised she should be so condescending.

The woman glanced at him uncertainly again. 'I might want a room for about a month, but,' pausing, she turned back to Stacy, 'my son might not be staying quite so long.'

'No longer than a week,' he said grimly. 'I'd like your best room for my mother, naturally.'

Why naturally? Looking at him sharply, Stacy suspected he was used to the best. He was arrogant and demanding, very sure of himself. Yet, in spite of his obvious sophistication, he had a healthy, vital, outdoor appearance. She continued to gaze at him, her curiosity surprisingly aroused at last. His mother seemed English, but Stacy instinctively sensed he didn't have an English father—or if he had, he hadn't been brought up in this country. Oh, well, her slender shoulders lifted wryly, what did it matter so long as they paid their bill? March could be an extremely bare month in the diary of a country guesthouse proprietor. Her mother would be glad to have them, no matter who they were.

The man's mother wandered back to the hall, leaving her son to sign the register. About to do this, he raised his dark, handsome head to stare at Stacy narrowly. 'You remind me of a girl I once dined with. She liked nothing on the menu, but took something rather than go hungry.'

Startled out of her indifference, Stacy blinked in confusion. 'I don't know what you mean,' she began.

'I think you do.' Any tolerance was gone, his voice hardened coldly. 'And I'm warning you. For my mother I not only want your best room, I want the best treatment. No little country girl adopts a couldn't-care-less attitude with either me or my family.'

Stacy had the grace to flush, while hiding the quick hate in her heart. 'I'm sorry,' her eyelids dropped as she strove to hide what she was thinking, 'I didn't mean to give such a bad impression. Perhaps it's because I don't usually work here.'

'And where you do, common politeness isn't a necessary qualification?'

'You're——' She had been about to say impertinent, but before his challenging stare her courage failed her. Instead she faltered, 'You're not all that polite yourself, are you?'

'But I don't have to be, do I, Miss Weldon? Seeing that I'm not on your side of the fence. Let me tell you I can be as polite as the next man when I have to be, but I'm quite capable of repaying your sort of behaviour in kind.'

'I—I didn't think I was being objectionable,' gasped Stacy, not really sure whether she had been or not. Inspiration struck as she found the thought of having this man in the house suddenly intolerable. Momentarily she forgot about her mother. 'There's a large hotel in town, not many miles away. It's big and modern, really smart. I'm sure it would be much more your style.'

'Really, miss?' Cold amusement added to the glitter already in his cold eyes. 'What makes you think you know me well enough to know what I like? I'm afraid I'm not interested in impersonal accommodation in the nearest city. When I return to Australia I want to be sure my mother is being looked after by people to whom she's not just a room number attached to a key. There are other reasons, but that's one of them, why I want to stay in a place like this. Maybe I could look further, though— there are bound to be other guesthouses in the district.'

So he was an Australian. She might have guessed. He had that look about him, she decided sourly, ignoring the fact that he was the first she had met. Reassessing swiftly, she recalled how he only wanted his room for a week. Then he would be returning to Australia, the other side of the world! Surely she—they could put up with him for that short a time, especially as it would mean having his mother much longer? Whatever his faults, she didn't doubt he would be prepared to pay generously for what he got, and it would make a good start to the tourist season, which was usually too short anyway.

Almost meekly she spoke. 'I'm sure when you meet my mother you'll be pleased, if you decide to stay here. She's much nicer than her daughter.' She stared rather desperately at the register as if willing now to humbly prostrate herself, if only he would sign.

'I hope I can believe it.'

Stacy's contrite mood almost deserted her at his contemptuous drawl. Her hand tightened unconsciously over the paperweight on which it was resting, but she restrained a foolish impulse to throw it. His glance, travelling slowly from her face to her hand, read her violent inclinations clearly. Coming back to linger on her face, as if to punish her, his eyes inspected, with unhurried insolence, every separate feature, before moving with an equal lack of haste down the slender curves of her young body. Then, quite unexpectedly, just when she was ready to see him throw down the pen and stride out, he bent and signed the register, a sardonic hint of satisfaction touching the corners of his well-cut mouth.

As he straightened, Stacy had to ignore the urge to turn the register around and study the names he had written there. All she could make out were the decisive strokes of a remarkably well formed hand.

'The name is Maddison.' Noting where she was looking, he twisted the book around in her direction, so she might see better. 'Sloan Maddison,' he continued, making her perusal seem irrelevant. 'My mother is Paula and we come from the Gulf country of Queensland, Australia. Do you know it?'

'No, I don't.' She glanced up at him, her very beautiful wide blue eyes tinged with an unconscious longing. 'I don't suppose I'll ever get the chance of seeing such far-away places.'

He made no comment on that, but kept staring at her

face. 'What's your name? Your Christian name, I mean?'

'Oh, I'm sorry.' She was letting herself drown in the dark glance he bent on her. With difficulty she wrenched her eyes away. 'I'm Stacy—Stacy Weldon.'

He inclined his head silently. 'Now perhaps you might care to show us what rooms you have to offer?'

'Yes. Yes, of course.' Feeling a stir of apprehension, Stacy slipped by him and led the way from the office. There wasn't much room and she was very conscious of his height and breadth. She wasn't fooled for a minute. Here was a man who would demand perfection in everything he touched. If the rooms upstairs didn't measure up, no signing of any register would persuade him to stay.

In the hall, Mrs Maddison was waiting and Stacy walked nervously in front of them, up the wide, curving staircase of which her mother had always been secretly rather proud. The house had been a farmhouse, well built, if rambling, and Stacy's father, when he had been alive, had farmed the not inconsiderable acreage which had gone with it. When he died the landlord had split the land among some of the smaller farms on the estate, but offered Mrs Weldon first refusal on the house. This she had managed to buy and equip as a guesthouse from the money which had been raised from the sale of stock and some which her father had left her years ago. It had been a struggle, but her eldest daughter, June, who had never trained for a career, had stayed and helped her, and together they had made a success of it. Thorn Farm, as it was still known, had slowly gathered a good reputation and was very popular.

Stacy, after recoving a little from being assaulted and then sacked from her job without a reference, had been determined to do everything she could to earn her keep. Not being able to bring herself yet to try and find another job, which might involve another boss like Basil Bradley, she had begged her mother to allow her to make a start on the redecoration of the bedrooms. As they were long overdue for it, Mrs Weldon had agreed. Two had already been completed, and Stacy knew without conceit that she had done an excellent job.

One was in a soft pink with toning colours beautifully blending. In the other she had used blue, which she'd never considered the easiest of colours to work with. It had taken every scrap of ingenuity, but the result was perfect. Both rooms had bathrooms attached, but while the pink had a bath, the blue had only a shower.

Mrs Maddison was clearly impressed. 'Oh, how delightful!' she exclaimed, her eyes absorbing the chintzy curtains and valances which Stacy had sewn herself. 'It's just the sort of thing, Sloan, I want for the Manor,' she rushed on, excitedly. Then, as her son quelled her exuberance with a glance, she sighed, speaking to Stacy more sedately, 'This will do very nicely, my dear. I'm sure it will suit me much better than a big hotel until I get...'

'Could I see my room, Miss Weldon?' Sloan Maddison asked.

Again Stacy wondered if he deliberately prevented his mother from finishing or if it had been merely boredom with such feminine frippery which had urged him to escape. The mention of a manor was mysterious, especially as Mrs Maddison seemed to give the impression that she might be moving somewhere. Whatever it was, Sloan Maddison was not going to encourage his mother to chat indiscriminately to a girl they scarcely knew.

'I'll just stay here, Sloan.'

'Yes, Paula.'

Stacy felt a hint of surprise that he should call his mother by her first name, but realised suddenly that she might not understand a man like this at all. For all her years at college and the one she had spent in London, she had never gathered any intimate knowledge of men. If she had she might have dealt better with Basil. Sloan Maddison, she sensed, would be way ahead of her in almost every experience she could think of.

The March wind blew coolly against the windows of the blue room and, although he seemed to approve of it, he had nothing to say.

'Don't you like it?' she burst out at last, feeling unbearably worried by his bored scrutiny. Something about this stranger was affecting her oddly. It was as if his cold eyes, intentionally or otherwise, seared her, melting her former indifference. Again she sensed his hard, vital masculinity and in her stomach curled an odd excitement.

'Sure,' he glanced at her with a look of cool amusement as he turned to find her at his shoulder, where, without intending to, she had allowed his silence to draw her. 'Is this a new angle, Miss Weldon? I've travelled fairly widely, but no one has ever been so interested in my opinion before. The most they've ever done was hope I would be comfortable.'

'I—I'm sorry,' What an unpleasant man! She couldn't wait to get downstairs to warn June! Again she had to swallow her irritation before making an effort, for her mother's sake. 'You'll find we believe in the personal touch here.'

'From the way you welcomed me,' he countered mockingly, 'I find that somewhat hard to believe. I feared I might be relegated to the chill of an attic. Between the doorstep and this bedroom something must have happened to make you change your mind.'

'I'm sure you're imagining things, Mr Maddison.' For the life of her Stacy couldn't keep a sudden sharpness from her voice, and she knew he was aware of it.

As if to taunt her, he smiled blandly, 'Just how far does this personal touch go?'

Because she didn't get his exact meaning, she couldn't answer but watched in silent bewilderment as he walked to the bed. He reminded her of a powerful, prowling animal, and this time the peculiar heat in her stomach seemed to spread to her limbs.

His strong legs touched the side of the bed as he glanced down at it. 'Changes of temperature do make a difference,' he mused, with apparent innocence. 'Do I get an electric blanket?'

'Yes. All you need do is tell us when you like it switched on?'

'I don't.'

'Don't?' Stacy queried.

'Like it switched on, Miss Weldon.' He might have been speaking to a particularly dense child. 'I prefer the human element or none at all.'

Quickly confused, she started, 'Of course, you're talking about your wife?'

'I'm not married, Miss Weldon.'

'Oh!' Her cheeks scorched with a sudden comprehending anger, as she met his expressionless eyes. 'I'm afraid we're not all that obliging!'

His eyes roamed her shabby sweater, and though they paused on the inviting peaks of her breasts, she fancied she saw only contempt in their dark depths. 'Really, Miss Weldon! A moment ago you were hinting at my imagination!'

Inside, Stacy felt provoked, almost beyond endurance. Here was a man who would twist words, and even actions, to suit his own ends. They would have been better off without him. She pitied his poor mother, who obviously had to do as she was told. Stacy's chin tilted defiantly as she stared at him. 'I beg your pardon,' she said, her tone denying any real apology.

Sloan Maddison fell silent for a second, then surprised her by merely asking curtly, 'Have you anyone to bring up our luggage?'

'We have an old man who comes for an hour or two most mornings.'

'Which isn't much use now, is it? What makes you think it's still morning?'

'What on earth are you talking about?' she gasped.

He stared intently, not apparently having any compunction about doing so. 'You said good morning when we arrived, and it's now two o'clock.'

'Oh?' Guilty colour stole into Stacy's pale cheeks. She was well aware that she didn't always take much notice of the time—at least, she hadn't lately. 'It's an easy enough mistake to make,' she defended herself.

'But not usual in girls of your age,' his eyes narrowed sardonically. 'It's often a sign of an unhappy love affair.'

'I don't have—love affairs, Mr Maddison.'

'Then maybe it's time you had. A lack of them seems to make some people just as unhappy.'

'Something you wouldn't know about, Mr Maddison!' she retorted, angry to feel she had gone so white.

'You keep jumping to conclusions about me,' he said gently, but with a hint of steel in his voice. 'I suppose speculating about your guests does help to enliven your day, but I warn you I don't altogether appreciate it.'

'Well, you were speculating about me first,' she mumbled sullenly, not caring for his astuteness.

'What a fiery young woman you are!' In a stride he was standing right beside her again, the sharp, clean scent of him tantalising her nostrils. Again he seemed to want to examine her closely, his hands going out to grasp her upper arms, to hold her still. He took in the startling blue of her eyes, her pale, rose-tinted, flawless complexion, the silky masses of red-gold hair, the way in which it flowed and curled over her shoulders, giving her small face every appearance of outraged elegance. Lastly his glance rested on her soft mouth, the sensuously curved fullness of it and, as if unable to resist it, his head bent and his mouth came down to cover hers with expert precision.

'No!' she cried, in the same moment as their lips met and shock waves sent her reeling. She felt, had he not been holding her, she might have fallen. The bedroom dissolved and everything in it. There was only the intimate touch of his hands drawing her closer, and her heart racing madly as a strange warmth began melting the ice in her veins. His arms tightened, and there was just the total unreality of whirling into endless space.

Then she was free. Free to draw the deep, sobbing breath of anger which had somehow got stuck in her throat. 'How dared you do that?' she gasped. 'We don't want your kind here. I'll have you thrown out!'

He was studying her throbbing red mouth with more interest than he seemed to be applying to her words. 'As your man only comes in the mornings, I don't see how you're going to manage it,' he drawled.

Mercifully, just when Stacy felt ready to give way to hysteria, or something worse, her mother arrived. Mrs Weldon didn't appear to notice anything unusual in her daughter's fluctuating colour and, after muttering a few barely comprehensible words of introduction, Stacy fled.

June, having just put her apple pie in the oven, was now busy chopping vegetables in the blender for soup. Raising her head from the carrots she was scraping at the sink, she turned as Stacy rushed in. 'Guess who rang?' she smiled happily. 'Richard's back.'

'He's beastly. Absolutely beastly!' Stacy gasped.

'Stacy!' June exclaimed, her expression as belligerent as it could get in one so placid. 'You know he isn't. I won't listen!'

'I'm not talking about Richard, silly. I'm glad he's home again, at least for your sake.'

'Then what. . . ?'

'Our new guest, upstairs! That is, he's beastly, not his mother.'

Patiently, June sighed, trying to sort this out. 'So it was people after rooms? The phone rang, you see, and I've only just left it, but Mum came in and I sent her up to see what you were doing.'

'She's upstairs with them now,' said Stacy.

'So what's the trouble? Small boys can be beastly, you know, but they're often the ones who grow up into the nicest men, the most loving ones, like Richard.'

Need June always be so—so physical? She and Richard loved each other and Stacy had a vague suspicion that they were already lovers. They were going to be married, which was perhaps just as well, as she had seen the way they looked at each other. 'This one upstairs is no schoolboy,' she spoke sharply, 'and I didn't take to him.'

'How come?'

'Because I didn't.' It wasn't much of an excuse, but now it came down to it, Stacy realised she couldn't possibly confess that Sloan Maddison, a perfect stranger, had kissed her.

'Well,' screamingly reasonable, as usual, June pointed out, 'you don't have to, do you? After all, he's just a guest, and all that's required is to be polite.'

'Even that might prove too much for me,' Stacy warned darkly.

'Stacy!' June hesitated, on a note of impatience. 'It doesn't do to imagine all men are alike. Just because Basil Bradley called you to his office after closing time and tried to assault you, it doesn't mean you can never trust another man again.'

'How can I, though?' Stacy retaliated, with angry tears. 'Shouldn't the fact that I was found half naked with Basil Bradley by his fiancée, and dismissed without a hearing just because she happens to be the chairman's daughter, be enough to stop a girl ever trusting a man again? Everything's gone—wasted! My training, my success as an interior decorator, both in London and here. All gone, overnight, along with my reputation. Shouldn't this be enough to make me bitter? I'd stopped counting the number of young couples who came to me, the colour schemes I'd worked out for them, the advice I was able to give on the decorating of their homes. I was good and becoming well known, even if I do say it myself. Now I know it won't ever happen again.'

'But it will! Of course it will! This is what I'm trying to tell you.'

'No, it won't,' Stacy's passionate young mouth set stubbornly. 'And I'd thank you not to keep on dragging it up, June. You know I hate talking about it.'

'That's half your trouble, I believe,' June sighed. 'You've never talked about it! It's like something you've tucked away, you're determined to keep out of sight. And,' more coldly, 'I do not keep on dragging it up! You know I don't. I think this is the first time I've mentioned it in weeks, and it's only for your own good. I believe it's time you began facing up to things, and learnt to live again. It's not as if Basil Bradley really hurt you in any way. Not in the way that matters.'

Her face white, Stacy acknowledged this, but whispered painfully, 'You know very well that some girls never get over the shock. I never thought you could be so cruel, June.'

'Cruel to be kind, I think.' Bluntly June tipped her vegetables into a pan of beef stock and replaced the blender. 'And if this man upstairs has helped wake you up, then I'm looking forward to meeting him.'

'I hope you aren't preparing to love him, just because he's upset me?'

'Don't be silly. I mean, he's a guest, isn't he? If there's one thing I've learnt about guests,' June said drily, 'it's not to love them. They're here today, gone tomorrow. They're usually seeking comfort, not love.'

'Some of the men could be.'

'Someone to have an illicit affair with, you mean?' June was always frank, if it wasn't going to hurt anybody. 'Well, maybe, but not usually with our sort of guests. The men who choose to stay at a very respectable country guesthouse generally have a wife in tow, or a fiancée.'

'When did that ever stop them?' Biting her lip, as her thoughts seemed naturally to gravitate towards Basil Bradley, Stacy wandered over to the window and stared out. The hateful memory of Basil's urgent hands on her bare flesh returned to horrify her and she scarcely heard June's rather helpless apology. If only she could forget! No man had ever touched her like that before. He had been like an animal, and she would never run the risk of it happening again. Not with Basil Bradley or any other man.

Before that, men had kissed her, but mostly they had been boys of around her own age. She'd usually enjoyed it, she had been to some parties where she had even gone a bit further than that, but she had never allowed anything in the way of real liberties. It had never, somehow, seemed worth it when she had felt nothing and had never liked a man enough to want to satisfy his lust. She thrust away the memory of the peculiar excitement aroused by Sloan Maddison, putting it down to panic and disgust.

Feeling June continuing to stare at her in anxious remorse, she managed to smile weakly and assure June that she was probably right and she would make a greater effort to pull herself together. June started to speak again, but was interrupted by the telephone, which could be heard ringing on one of the extensions outside. She went to answer it.

Stacy went on gazing out of the window. It began to rain and she watched the raindrops pattering on the old roof of the converted garages in the yard, darkening the slate before reaching the gutters. Because March, in England, was capable of producing almost everything in the way of weather, snowflakes fell in the rain, and although she could see it wouldn't be much, she wished angrily that it might be enough to send Sloan Maddison hurrying back to where he came from. You could tell he was used to a much warmer climate than this. It stood out a mile in the bronzed tan of his skin, the hard, outdoor appearance of him.

There had been a girl in the London store where Stacy had worked before coming back to Birmingham. She had been as brown as a berry, as she had just come from Australia, and talked a lot about the wonderful beaches and the vitality of the men. She had spent a holiday in Queensland, where the Maddisons had come from. It had been on an island on the Great Barrier Reef, if Stacy remembered correctly. Lydia had said it was gorgeous. Eventually she had returned to live there permanently.

Reflectively, Stacy rubbed her fingers along the broad, white-painted windowsill, not realising what she was doing until she encountered a rough splinter. Frowning, as she sucked a speck of blood from her finger in her mouth, she looked closely at the wood. It was in need of attention, and as it would be almost impossible to continue in the bedrooms with visitors staying, maybe she could make a start here. It would be a pity to waste all her extensive training, and this did need a coat of paint, if nothing else. Besides, she was very fond of the old farmhouse where she had been born, and felt she wanted to help look after it.

Wistfully her eyes penetrated the stone walls of the yard outside, seeing clearly, as though she had been standing in them, the surrounding fields and woods, the unhurried streams and rivers which were so much a fundamental part of the English countryside. Would she ever willingly exchange this for any of Lydia's sun-baked beaches? She did wish, though, that Thorn Farm had never needed to be turned into a guesthouse. If only Daddy had still been alive. He had been an excellent farmer and the farm had paid well, well enough to give his wife plenty of the good things in life and his two daughters a boarding school education. What a waste it seemed that he had had to die so young! Now the land was sold and Stacy was no longer the daughter of a prosperous farmer.

The door behind her opened and when her mother came in she was smiling. 'What a nice couple! Well, they're hardly that, but you know what I mean.'

'She's nice, he isn't,' said Stacy, without hesitation.

Mrs Weldon didn't look too surprised, understanding her daughter's present frame of mind. 'Just so long as you keep your temporary dislike of men to yourself, darling, I won't argue, but I personally think the son's rather dishy!'

'Oh, Mums, you're nearly fifty!'

'Good heavens, child, what has that got to do with it? Age doesn't deprive one of the ability to appreciate good looks.'

'I suppose not,' Stacy shrugged awkwardly.

'If it comes to that,' said her mother dreamily, 'Mr Maddison can't be so very young himself. I should think he's at least thirty-five or six.'

'Possibly.' Stacy frowned, appreciating her mother still looked young and pretty but hoping she wasn't getting any strange ideas.

'I wonder what brings them here?' Mrs Weldon wandered over to the big Aga cooker and lifted the lid from the pan of soup June was making. Sniffing appreciatively, she reached for a spoon and gave it a quick stir before tasting. Stacy could tell by her movements that her mind was not completely on what she was doing. 'It does seem a bit odd, coming all that way to stay here at this time of year, from a cattle station in Australia. Your father used to talk about these huge landowners over there. I believe he had a cousin who once worked for one. They own millions of acres and make a lot of money and like touring the world, I suppose, spending it. But there can't be much to see here.'

Unimpressed, Stacy grimaced. 'Just because he has a farm, or something, in the wilds of Australia, it doesn't necessarily mean he's a millionaire.'

'Maybe not, but you should see their luggage and their car! Yes, I know the car will be hired, but you can always tell. It's in Mr Maddison's manner, that indefinable something. We got around a lot, you know, your father and I. I learnt how to judge a man, if nothing else.'

'But, as you say, there can't be much for people like the Maddisons here.' Stacy was suspicious rather than particularly curious. 'Maybe they have relations in the district, or are searching through churchyards for long-dead ancestors. A lot of people from all over the world come here to do that.'

'Quite,' Mrs Weldon agreed drily. 'Only he doesn't seem the type who would spare the time.'

'He'd be more interested in the living,' Stacy mumbled darkly, recalling the vital strength of his arms.

Mrs Weldon didn't appear to be listening. 'He doesn't seem the sort who usually travels with his mother, either.'

'No consideration,' said Stacy scornfully. 'I can just see him pushing her out, sending the poor woman off to fend for herself.'

'Really, Stacy!' Mrs Weldon blinked, as if only just realising her daughter's antipathy. 'You seem to have reached an awful lot of adverse conclusions in a very short time.'

'Perhaps you aren't the only one who's good at weighing men up.' Then, as her mother blinked again, apprehensively, Stacy sighed. 'Oh, well, what does it matter? Do they happen to want afternoon tea?'

'No, they have to go out. They've already gone, actually, to see someone in Birmingham. They didn't say what about, of course, but they'll be in for dinner.'

'So we have that grain of information, at least.' Stacy paused, aware of being childish but unable to restrain herself. 'Do you know, he never said his room was nice, and I spent so much time over it. I had to ask if he was satisfied, and then he was only sarcastic.'

'Well, dear,' Mrs Weldon shot Stacy a puzzled look, 'men don't always notice such things. His mother did, though,' she added quickly. 'Mrs Maddison was still in raptures as they went out, but do you see what I mean about money? A man like Mr Maddison, who's obviously been born to it, will always take such perfection for granted.'

'He might find one day his money won't buy everything.' Stacy moved from the window to join her mother beside the cooker.

Mrs Weldon sighed, her face assuming a patience which reminded Stacy too much of June's. 'Never mind, darling. Just as long as he has enough to pay for what he gets here, I don't think we should concern ourselves over-much about the state of his finances. Now I wonder if you could go and find June for me. If we don't get tonight's menu sorted out soon, we might have to give the Maddisons egg sandwiches, and that would never do!'

Betty, their mainstay from the nearby village during the summer months, had heard somehow about the new guests and rang to ask if they would need her. Later it transpired that it was her mother who had directed the Maddisons to Thorn Farm. Rather uncertainly Stacy agreed that she should come. She was sure she and June could have managed, but she didn't want to do Betty out of her job, especially when she might not be here much longer herself. Not once she'd got herself properly sorted out and found some fresh work. As Mrs Maddison was hovering in the hall, obviously with an enquiry, she rang off, after telling Betty to come about seven.

Feeling rather guilty, she found her mother and told her about Betty, but Mrs Weldon agreed that Stacy had done the right thing. As she would be out herself that evening, she could relax, knowing that Betty was in charge of the dining room, even if there were to be only two guests. Under Betty's proven expertise, nothing disastrous was likely to happen, and it was always nice to make a good impression, especially with people from overseas. It was amazing how good reputations could be ruined almost overnight by the merest hint of bad service. Stacy had been so absentminded lately, she couldn't really be trusted not to drop something.

Aware from Stacy's anxious expression that she had guessed what she was thinking, Mrs Weldon looked faintly apologetic, but didn't actually say she was sorry.

'If I hadn't promised to give this talk to the Women's Institute, we might have done the job between us, but it wouldn't be fair to let them down at the last minute. Besides, we'll probably be full up again by this time next month, and this will give Betty a chance to get her hand in.'

CHAPTER TWO

STACY, trying to shrug off a distinct feeling of failure, nodded without replying. She understood her mother's motives too well to be critical. They were very convenient for Stratford-on-Avon, with its famous theatre and Shakespearean plays which drew countless tourists every summer, and during the next four or five months Mrs Weldon must make enough to keep herself during the following winter. This, along with the necessary cleaning, redecoration and repairs, made a good season absolutely essential. Not for the first time, Stacy realised her mother's life must be far from easy.

As Mrs Weldon had read history at university, she was to speak on the Kings and Queens of England. After wishing her luck and seeing her off, Stacy helped June serve dinner. Before dinner she had caught a brief glimpse of Sloan Maddison, darkly formidable in an impeccably tailored business suit, on his way to the dining room. Fortunately she had had time to dodge behind a door until he'd passed. She had caught a glimpse, too, of Betty's rather dazzled face as she had followed him in.

Tonight Stacy felt a little wary about being alone with June. June was five years older, and subsequently thought she was wiser, and it was obvious she had decided a change of tactics was what was needed to jerk Stacy from her continuing lethargy. In fact, Stacy knew that the shock she had suffered at Basil Bradley's hands was beginning to subside to a dull ache, and what June didn't seem to understand was that her well-intentioned prodding was bringing it alive again.

Betty had asked to be away early, also to a prearranged date, and Stacy had promised she would see to coffee.

'Why don't you take it in?' June, having stacked the dishwasher, turned it on as she glanced up at Stacy. The coffee cups were of a beautiful hand-painted china, and she preferred to wash these by hand.

'Me?' exclaimed Stacy in confusion, with perhaps more feeling than was necessary. She had been thinking of Sloan Maddison and Betty's admiring remarks, which had been flowing thick and fast all evening. Because of this, after proclaiming her dislike of him, Stacy felt strangely guilty.

'Yes, you!' June watched Stacy's uncertain face with fresh impatience. 'You know we love you, darling, but you really will have to make an effort to pull yourself together!' Her voice rose sharply, to fill the kitchen. 'What you really need is a short but devastating affair with a man who knows what he's doing. Why, girls of your age are often hopping in and out of men's beds regularly, and thinking nothing of it. You're such a little prude!'

'Excuse me.'

The dry, masculine voice spun both girls around like tops. June recovered first, after casting a remorseful glance at Stacy. 'Good evening, Mr Maddison. Stacy was just about to bring your coffee, if this is what you happen to be looking for. I'm afraid I have to go out.'

Sloan Maddison showed his appreciation of June's charming smile with one of his own, which changed his austere appearance so much that Stacy almost gasped. But it was at Stacy he looked when he spoke again. 'I wasn't actually looking for anything. My mother wondered if you would care to join her for coffee, and your waitress seems to have disappeared.'

'Oh,' meeting his intent gaze head on, Stacy heard herself stammering, 'I—I don't know if I could.'

'Why not? It might be a good idea, if your sister is going out and you're to be alone.'

'Of course she'll go,' said June, with another naturally charming smile at Sloan Maddison. 'It will make a nice change.'

Sloan Maddison's dark brows rose slightly but he had no comment to make on that. 'I'll have my coffee later, if you don't mind, and it would greatly oblige me if you would keep my mother company.' He was looking directly at Stacy again, but she found it impossible to sustain his speculative gaze. 'I've made arangements with your mother to use the office—I have some calls to make to Australia which I'm afraid may take some time.'

Stacy, wondering how much he had overheard of June's questionable advice, nodded her beautiful head, knowing she couldn't reasonably avoid doing as he asked. She would rather that June had been able to accompany her, but Richard was picking her up in a few minutes. How Stacy wished she had an excuse, as the others had. Something about Sloan Maddison made her wish only to avoid him.

'I won't be a moment,' she murmured, her cheeks pink as she recalled their previous encounter. She wondered how he had the nerve to stand staring at her so contemplatively. If he had heard something of what June had been saying, he could be feeling curious, but he had no need to concern himself over something which was none of his business.

Leaving June, who had met him earlier, and who was almost as impressed as Betty, chatting to him happily, Stacy escaped into the scullery behind the kitchen, to remove her overall. Under it she wore only a thin green body shirt as the kitchen grew so hot when June was cooking, but Stacy scarcely paused to consider her appearance. After quickly washing her hands she smoothed in a little scented lotion, then tried to comb her hair. Unfortunately the thickness of it had tangled while she had been working and she had to give up. The result in the small, rusty mirror which hung there was charming, but not as neat as she would have liked. With a rueful sigh she replaced the comb and went back to the kitchen.

The kitchen was large and warm and very attractive. While it had had to be modernised to conform to present-day catering standards, they had managed to do this without losing too much of the old character. A minute ago Stacy had heard Richard's car drive up and she was not surprised to find Sloan Maddison alone. He was gazing around with marked appreciation when Stacy reappeared, but he said nothing, merely inclined his head and picked up the coffee tray which she had prepared earlier.

'Lead the way,' he commanded, ignoring her quick protest as he motioned for her to precede him. 'I'm quite capable of carrying one tray of coffee.'

Mrs Maddison was waiting in the drawing room, which was a pretty room, combining elegance with comfort. Usually Mrs Weldon used another lounge for her paying guests, keeping this one for the family. That she was allowing the Maddisons to share this privilege Stacy found somewhat disturbing, especially when she wasn't sure Sloan Maddison would appreciate such an honour. She had a feeling he was slightly irritated by the necessity of having to make this visit and was only acting from a sense of duty.

Mrs Maddison, looking extremely elegant in a long smart dress, made Stacy immediately conscious of her own shorter skirt, even though it was of fine, soft wool and matched the green of her top. Rather guiltily her thoughts dwelt on the number of smart, flowing evening gowns she had upstairs. Yet wouldn't it have seemed slightly ridiculous to have got all dressed up, just to have coffee with a tourist? Mrs Maddison might have thought so, too.

As they entered the room Mrs Maddison glanced up from the magazine she was reading and smiled as Stacy said good evening to her and pulled forward a table to receive the tray her son was carrying. If Mrs Maddison was sur-

prised to see him performing such a task she gave no indication.

'I'll be back, just as soon as I'm through,' he told his
mother, and after another long, enigmatical glance at Stacy's
slightly mutinous face, left them.

Inexplicably Stacy found herself staring after him, as
if she could follow his progress through the closed door.
Her heart was thumping strangely and she felt as though
she had been running a long way.

'Do sit down, dear. You can pour my coffee.'

Stacy started at Mrs Maddison's calm voice and smiled
apologetically, 'Yes, of course.'

'Some for yourself, too. Is your sister joining us?'

'I'm afraid she's gone out.' Stacy passed the sugar. 'Her
fiancé called for her.'

Mrs Maddison didn't appear too disappointed. She took
two spoonfuls of sugar, stirring it into her coffee thought-
fully. 'And your mother's gone, too, although she explained.
Don't you go out yourself of an evening, Miss Weldon?'

'No, you see—— Well, no, I haven't been out much
lately, anyway.' Stacy pulled herself up sharply, aghast to
suspect she had been about to confide something of her
unhappy circumstances. Rather warily her blue eyes flick-
ered. Like her son, something about Paula Maddison
seemed to reach out and touch her, although Mrs Maddison communicated with an entirely different part of her.
Stacy was aware of some vague thread of sympathy between herself and this woman. It was weak as yet, but instinctively she felt it could grow stronger. She was suddenly
sure Paula Maddison had liked her instantly, in spite of
Stacy's less than welcoming attitude when the Maddisons
had first arrived, and Stacy surprisingly felt a similar regard stirring within her.

Mrs Maddison looked curiously at Stacy's taut face,
but all she said was, 'In the Outback, where we live, a girl
has to get used to staying in. We do visit a lot, it's much
easier, nowadays, when we have our own private planes,

and there are parties and picnic race meetings and such like, but most of the time a girl stays at home.'

'You must be very isolated and lonely.'

'Not really. There are plenty of things to do, it all depends what you like. There's horse riding and swimming and,' drily, 'of course work. We do a lot of that. It might be rewarding, but it's a very hard life. Sloan, my son, works all the hours God sends and then some, though he wouldn't thank me for mentioning it.'

As Stacy sought to grasp this, Mrs Maddison said briskly, 'So you don't go out at nights. What do you do through the day? Help mother, or do you have another job?'

'Not—not at the moment, Mrs Maddison.' In her imagination, Stacy had been riding horses, something she loved doing, over endless plains, and she hated to be jerked from such an enticing vista, to be brought back to earth in this way.

'Your mother was telling me that you're a properly trained interior decorator, that it was you who'd done such a wonderful job upstairs.'

'Yes,' Stacy agreed nervously. She didn't know what her mother had told Mrs Maddison, but she didn't want to talk about her career, not when Sloan Maddison might return at any minute. Grasping at anything to change the subject, she asked quickly, 'Are you on a world tour, Mrs Maddison?'

'No,' Paula Maddison temporised, with a quick glance towards the door, which seemed to confirm Stacy's earlier suspicions that Sloan Maddison didn't want his mother talking indiscreetly. 'We only left home last week. We did two stopovers, as Sloan said it was too far for me to attempt in one go, but we certainly aren't doing any world tour. From April to October, you see, is our busiest time on the station and Sloan would like to get back as soon as possible.'

As Paula paused, Stacy watched her curiously. Again

it came to her that Mrs Maddison might almost have been born in this country. 'Are you English?' she asked, marvelling at her own temerity.

Mrs Maddison laughed, smoothing a hand over her well groomed grey hair, her eyes twinkling. 'English, Australian, my dear, is there much real difference? But yes, I was born in this country and lived here until I met and married Sloan's father, who was a commissioned officer in the last war. He was wounded and I was a nurse and we fell in love. He didn't give me much time to think about it. In little over a week after he left hospital, we were married and on our way to his cattle station in Queensland, where his ancestors had been among the first settlers. Sloan was born in 1945 and is exactly like his father was when it comes to getting what he wants.'

Stacy shuddered, not finding this at all difficult to believe. Paula Maddison's story intrigued her. 'Your husband?' she asked tentatively.

'I'm a widow, like your mother,' Paula sighed. 'I'm afraid my husband never completely recovered from his war wounds. He died when Sloan was fifteen.'

'I see,' Stacy nodded, feeling the link of sympathy growing stronger, as she caught the brief glimpse of sadness in Paula's eyes.

'You're a strange girl.' Paula suddenly looked at her warmly. 'Do you know, I feel I can talk to you better than to my own family, either my son or daughter.'

So Sloan had a sister? Surely there couldn't be anyone else quite like him? So startled was she at such a possibility, Stacy wasn't prepared to find Mrs Maddison leaning forward and saying, in a low voice, 'I'm going to tell you a secret. The reason I'm here is because I've been left a small manor house in the district and I want to come and live in it.'

'You mean you want to leave your Australian home, where you've lived all this time?' Stacy sounded very young in her unconscious disapproval and Paula smiled slightly at her startled surprise.

'I don't particularly want to leave it, dear. It's just that, since this legacy cropped up, I've decided I'd rather spend my remaining years here. It could never be an easy choice, but since my husband died nothing at Taronda seems to have been the same.'

'Taronda?'

'The station.'

'Oh.' Stacy hesitated, feeling as if she was drowning in a sea of unexpected information and not yet very sure of her facts. Mrs Maddison was obviously suffering from the very human need to talk to someone. Stacy hoped she wouldn't live to rue the day, if her son got to hear how she had confided in a near stranger! Gulping, as she guessed Sloan Maddison very capable of anger, she said quickly, 'But you must have a lot of happy memories tied up in Taronda?'

'Both good and bad,' Paula sighed. 'Somehow I've never been able to decide whether Taronda is the end of the world or out of this world. It's a place you can both love and hate. I reared two children on it and lost two babies because of it—the first because the weather was so wet the Flying Doctor couldn't reach us, the next for the same reason, but because of bush fire.'

'How terrible!' exclaimed Stacy, in a kind of daze of compassion. It cut her own troubles down to size just thinking about it.

Paula shrugged, although the momentary sadness came back to her eyes. 'That was life in the Outback, dear, everyone accepted it. It's not quite so bad today, but there are still plenty of hazards. It rather depends on the kind of man you have in charge. Sloan, now, he's the sort of man everyone relies on, from the top man right down to the smallest Abo.'

'Abo?' Stacy glanced at Mrs Maddison reluctantly, not

really wanting to hear her continue praising her son, but feeling curious all the same.

'Aborigine, dear. We have quite a few Aborigine stockmen, and you couldn't get better. A lot of them have their wives and families on the station and, of course, they're all to look after. Sloan is good and kind to them all, all the stockmen, both black and white, but he rules with a rod of iron, and there's not one who dares step out of line.'

Apprehensively, Stacy swallowed, not finding this too difficult to believe. Hadn't she been exposed to the edge of his overbearing arrogance herself? 'Wouldn't your son miss you, if you came to live here? Would his sister be willing to look after him?'

'Sally is married and living in Sydney, but we do have a housekeeper. No, Sloan wouldn't miss me.'

What an awful admission for any mother to have to make! If it was true, Stacy couldn't believe it could be Mrs Maddison's fault. 'You could be mistaken. How can you be so sure?'

Mrs Maddison looked at her and sighed, as if relating facts she had long learnt to live with. 'Sloan is a law unto himself, my dear, quite independent of me or anyone. I suppose he had to grow up too quickly when his father died— but then it takes a man to manage Taronda. He outgrew me long ago, although I know he will always want to assure himself that I'm all right. And one of these days he might marry and his wife might not really want me. I'd be much better to make the break now, while I'm still young enough and have the chance.'

Stacy found herself considering this more closely than she liked. 'Is there someone he has already in mind? A girl he's definitely decided to marry?'

'Not exactly. I'm not really sure. There's plenty he could have for the asking,' Paula said tartly. 'He has said he'll have to marry some time, if only for the sake of the station. Otherwise it would go to a cousin's son, whom he can't stand the sight of.'

'Dear me,' exclaimed Stacy, very soberly, 'I do feel sorry for him.'

Paula glanced at her a trifle suspiciously, but finding nothing to suggest anything but respect, she frowned. 'So you do understand why I feel I must leave Taronda.'

Still not sure that she did, Stacy suggested something else. 'You could be lonely. Do you have any other relations over here besides the one who died and left you his house? That is,' she paused awkwardly, 'I'm presuming it was a relative who left it to you.'

'It was a relative,' Paula nodded her head, 'and I have quite a few left; they only need looking up. Sloan thinks I may have been away too long and they might not be so pleased to see me.'

'Mr Maddison isn't exactly encouraging, is he?' Stacy commented drily. 'I gather he doesn't altogether approve of your coming to the Midlands to live.'

'No, I'm afraid he doesn't. He would rather I was where he could check exactly what I was up to—which won't be very easy from the other side of the world.'

Stacy couldn't argue with that and she glanced at Mrs Maddison uneasily. She detected a note of triumph in her voice which she didn't understand, and hoped suddenly that she knew what she was doing. 'I—I don't suppose you would want to antagonise your son completely?' she said, having some vague notion of pouring oil on troubled waters.

'I'll just have to hope he comes around,' Paula closed the subject lightly. 'Now I was going to ask you about the manor. Would you care to come with me tomorrow to see it?'

Stacy felt rather taken aback. 'Whereabouts is it?' she hedged, to avoid an immediate decision.

'Just down the road from here—Bilton Manor.' Paula's face changed eagerly. 'I should think you must know it?'

'Bilton Manor?' Stacy's face lit up, too, but with astonishment. She should know where it was as it lay only about a mile the other side of the village. It stood back from the road, but so far as she could tell, the house was boarded up. 'Yes, I know where it is,' she said quickly, 'but I can't remember anyone ever living there. I believe there was an old gentleman ...'

'My mother's cousin. I can quite believe you wouldn't know him as he's lived in a home for the past twenty years, which must have been since about the time you were born. He was almost a hundred when he died and I'm afraid I'd completely forgotten his existence—or if I did remember him it was only to imagine he'd died long ago. It makes me feel terribly ashamed, now that I've learnt otherwise, that I never took the trouble to look him up. I could have done, as I've visited England several times. This is one of the reasons why I'd especially like to keep his house, since he was kind enough to leave it to me. Of course, it will be a while yet before it could be fit to live in as it's been closed up for so long, but we have an architect coming over tomorrow.' She lay back in her chair, as if her lengthy speech had exhausted her. 'He's to go over it thoroughly, but I would appreciate it if you would agree to come too, just to have a look at the rooms with me. You might be able to help me decide whether there's any possibility of making it into an attractive home. I know if there's no one there besides myself, Sloan will take one look at it and write it off. You've no idea what he can do with a few well chosen words, once he gets started!'

If nothing else might have persuaded Stacy, this did! That, and the chance of being able to allow her imagination the freedom of a whole house. Never before had she been offered such an opportunity. Interest flowed, glowing in her cheeks, almost washing out the blight of Basil Bradley. 'I'd love to come, Mrs Maddison. That is,' she hesitated, not quite so bravely, 'if you're sure Mr Maddison won't object too strongly?'

'If I don't object to what, Miss Weldon?'

Stacy nearly jumped out of her skin, as Sloan Maddison spoke. This was the second time in one evening! If he hadn't been a guest she would have accused him of creeping up on people. She hadn't even heard the door opening. Startled, she stared at him, as she swung her head around, her eyes becoming trapped by his dark gaze, so that for a moment she seemed deprived of the power to answer. He had removed his jacket, in the warmth of the central heating, and loosened his tie. She had to take a deep breath, as her pulse began its funny little tripping again. 'Mrs Maddison has just asked me to go with you—I—er—mean her—tomorrow, to see Bilton Manor. And I've agreed,' she proclaimed, with a kind of defiant glare, aimed more, she was ashamed to realise, to annoy him than please his mother.

Very coolly he replied, as he advanced into the room, still holding her gaze, like some sleek, predatory animal, biding its time. 'I'm sure you realise my mother is tired, Miss Weldon, and in the morning will probably regret involving a stranger in her affairs. Come the morning, too, I'm sure you'll find you have better things to do than involving yourself in the dubious pleasure of looking over a crumbling old house.'

'Oh, but it will be a pleasure, Mr Maddison, have no doubt about that. It certainly won't be any bother!' Stacy allowed her smile to widen brilliantly, certain, from the glint in his eye, that she was managing to irritate him. In that moment he wasn't a guest, prepared to pay quite handsomely for the privilege of staying in her mother's house, he was just a man who, somehow or another, aroused Stacy's deepest antagonism.

His black eyes studied her, drove into her, making her tremble, in spite of her bravado. It came to her suddenly that he might have some power over her, this man with the hard, dark eyes, should he care to exercise it. Perhaps she might be wise to take heed of some of the things his mother said about him.

While she floundered on the relevance of such a thought, Sloan Maddison turned to his mother, who was sitting frowning uncertainly. Although she had looked almost as startled as Stacy when he had come in, she made no obvious attempt to placate him. Rather she looked like someone carefully planning the next move.

With a complete blankness of expression, Sloan Maddison paused beside his mother's chair, looking down on her. 'You must be tired, Paula, so why not have an early night? I'll not be long in following you, unless I fall asleep down here, after Miss Weldon has seen to my coffee.'

Stacy, about to make her escape as well, halted in dismay. Damn the man—she was sure he didn't really want any!

Hopefully she glanced at Mrs Maddison, but found no help there. Mrs Maddison didn't appear to object to being pushed off to bed, for this was what it amounted to, but about her mouth was a faint line of stubbornness, as if she had decided she would stick to her own decisions about tomorrow and was far from defeated yet!

'Is there anything I can get you, Mrs Maddison?' Stacy asked gently, trying to convey her sympathy.

'I don't think so, dear, thank you.' Mrs Maddison swept out with a regal goodnight to Sloan.

It came to Stacy suddenly that mother and son were more alike than she had thought.

The coffee was cold. As she stood considering it uncertainly, Sloan Maddison helped himself to quite a large whisky. Presumably her mother had given him the run of the house. 'Do you really want coffee?' She tried to keep her voice even, so as not to incite him into saying yes, just to spite her.

'I do.' He tossed back his whisky. 'If that lot's cold hadn't we better adjourn to the kitchen to make some more? I'm sure ten-thirty isn't your regular bedtime.'

Nor your poor mother's, she felt like retorting, but the

look in his eye quelled her, as he read her thoughts correctly.

He followed her through the door, this time making no effort to carry the tray, as if he considered that with her hands full she couldn't escape him. 'I want to speak to you, and Paula is tired,' He opened the kitchen door, standing back to allow her through, as he added quite civilly, 'If I confess to a little manoeuvring, it was partly necessary, for her own good.'

Stacy set down her tray, smiling sharply. 'I'm sure you always act with this in mind, Mr Maddison, no matter whom you're dealing with.'

'If I were to put you over my knee, you mightn't find it so easy to be agreeable,' he drawled. 'When I first came here I never dreamt I'd have to deal with a girl like you, that's for sure!' Speaking between his teeth, he picked up the kettle and thrust it under the cold tap. 'Would you mind if I had tea instead of coffee?' His tone declared that whether she did or not, he was having it. 'I often make tea at home, last thing. It helps me sleep better.'

Her eyes widened with a kind of helpless, very young defiance. 'I shouldn't have thought anything, not even a cup of coffee, would have dared prevent you from sleeping, Mr Maddison!'

Calmly he turned off the tap, then placed the kettle on the hot-plate of the cooker. 'Now you're being childish.'

'Just because I have you weighed up?'

He turned from the stove so quickly she gasped, as his hands closed ruthlessly over her arms. 'Don't make the mistake of thinking you know me, Stacy, not in a few hours. I should warn you, it won't wash.'

Her voice squeaked infuriatingly as she met the contained blaze in his dark eyes. 'Well, you shouldn't insult me!'

'By suggesting you were being childish?'

'I'm not a child!'

He laughed suddenly, his teeth gleaming strong and white in the harsh twist of his lips. 'Honey, it's when I start thinking of you as being properly grown up that you can really begin to take fright.'

With an odd perverseness she exclaimed, 'I do happen to be nearly twenty-one, and have held down a job which involved quite a lot of responsibility. You can scarcely call that not being grown up?'

'Why should you want to convince me?' His hands slid to her shoulders as he turned her towards the light, to study her more closely. 'Perhaps you wouldn't have to try that hard, Miss Stacy Weldon. If it's compliments you're after, and what woman isn't, I think you're the most perfect young thing I've seen in a long time. But you notice how I emphasise your youth, in spite of your protests. You are young—too young for me, I'm thinking, and too beautiful for your own good.'

His eyes slid over her face, lingering on the mouth he had kissed only hours before, before moving to where her breasts thrust against the softness of her body shirt. Under his shirt sleeves she could see the muscles of his arms rippling. Dazed, as her glance came back to watch his assessing face, her eyes grew dreamy, her eyelids strangely heavy. She actually found herself swaying towards him.

'I . . .' she heard her own faint murmur of protest, as his mouth came down on her softly parted lips with a curiously pagan compulsion which made her want to cling. At the touch of his mouth she felt a sweet, intolerable weakness, she felt like a straw on the wind, floating, without identity. She couldn't tell what it was for she had never known anything like it. There was only the incredible sensation of being swept by a tornado and whirled to dizzying heights. His arms went around her, momentarily he crushed her tighter, then he was putting her firmly away from him.

His eyes mocked her disbelieving, faintly shocked expression. 'Perhaps I feel the same way, Stacy Weldon. The first time I'll admit to kissing you. This time I believe you asked for all you got, but no one in their right senses allows their emotions to get out of control within the first few hours of meeting someone.'

'Isn't it possible?' she whispered, still slightly dizzy, still not quite back to earth. His kiss had been brief, but she could still feel its swift intensity on her throbbing mouth.

'The older you get the more you realise anything's possible,' he said darkly, 'but in this case the answer is definitely no. My own life at the moment is too cluttered with minor irritations to look for more. I can well do without the help of a stubborn little English girl in complicating it any further, especially one as innocent as you.'

This, seeming more like an insult than a compliment, was immediately resented. Stacy's wide brows drew together in a frown. What he said might be true, but he had a very high-handed way with him which made her feel cold all over. She couldn't be held responsible for the briefness of their acquaintance, nor the way in which they seemed to react to each other. Nor did he have any grounds to justify his hint that she had become another of his minor irritations. She had only tried to answer his mother's obvious cry for help. Surely he couldn't hold that against her?

'Stacy,' he said, as though impatient with her frowning silence and the things he could see going through her head, 'I heard what your sister was saying, that you should have an affair. You aren't thinking of following her advice?'

Stacy flushed, relief washing strangely through her that he hadn't apparently overheard everything June had said. Otherwise, she guessed instinctively, his temper would have been slightly different. Even so, he couldn't possibly be imagining she would want an affair with him! He was the last man—and he had no need to be standing over her with such a superior look on his face.

Stiffly she drew away from him. 'Certainly not! But

sometimes I think I annoy June. You see, she and Richard
are engaged and sometimes I think she thinks I'm missing
out ...'

'I think I understand.' As Stacy's uncertain explanation
faltered to a halt, he spoke quietly, if with a hint of sardonic amusement. 'It can be extremely annoying to feel
someone is sitting in judgement on you, and you can provoke, Stacy Weldon, I'll say that for you.'

Unhappily, Stacy moved away from him. The last thing
she had intended was to call attention to June and Richard,
or to imply any criticism even indirectly, as there couldn't
be two nicer people. Her face paled as she hated Basil
Bradley afresh for the upheaval he had brought to her
previously smoothly running life, but she knew if she did
tell Sloan Maddison everything he would only, like June,
tell her to pull herself together and get on with it. There
would be little sympathy in this man for a girl who had
allowed herself to be so disorganised by something which
had never really happened. If he would believe Basil had
never actually harmed her in that way.

For the first time it struck Stacy that one day it could
be very important to be able to prove her innocence to
somone other than herself. Her family believed her, but
what if there was ever someone who mattered even more
than either June or her mother? Somehow Stacy hadn't
thought of this, and she found herself growing even
colder than she had done a moment ago. How could a man
like Sloan Maddison, whom she was never likely to see
again after the next few days, have prompted such a
thought?

'I never intended to provoke,' she cried, so vehemently
that it narrowed Sloan Maddison's eyes. But she was remembering how Basil Bradley had spoken almost those
very words to her, accusingly, after he had called her to
his office and tried to make love to her. In the struggle
which had followed, when he had torn her blouse, he had

accused her several times of this, and worse. He had so obviously been seeking for something to justify his attack that nothing had been gained by Stacy's hysterical declaration of the truth, that she had never so much as given him a second thought, let alone tried to encourage him in any way!

'Men like to imagine a girl provokes,' she added bitterly, 'when it helps to ease their conscience.'

Sloan's dark eyes gleamed as they rested on her full, soft mouth. 'With all your talk of equality, these days, why should a man be unduly worried by his conscience?'

Something in his eyes made her feel endangered. There was something too discerning in his scrutiny. 'But you're still the stronger sex, physically.'

A glint of amusement replaced his quizzical investigation. 'Mostly,' he agreed laconically. 'Maybe men should get down on their knees that there's something women can't change. No matter how hysterical you get about equal rights, you can never do much about that.'

'I suppose not,' she conceded grudgingly, never wanting to change anything but too ruffled to admit it.

'Now,' he suggested lightly, though his eyes were still intent on her disturbed but beautiful face, 'I propose we get down to talking about my mother.'

CHAPTER THREE

'YOUR mother?' Stacy, ashamed to find she had forgotten Mrs Maddison, gave a small start of surprise.

'When I said I wanted to talk to you, you must have guessed it was to do with my mother.'

'I wasn't sure.'

Sloan Maddison's mouth tightened before her assumed innocence. He rejoined sarcastically, 'If I'd wanted to discuss our very adequate accommodation, I'd have sought your mother. If I'd wanted to tour the surrounding countryside I should have consulted the local tourist office or maps.'

'You've only talked about—about ourselves,' Stacy protested mutinously, hoping to irritate him so much he might decide to go to bed. She didn't want to talk about Mrs Maddison, as she was sure this would involve the Manor house, and Stacy did want to see it. Sloan Maddison, she felt certain, was going to forbid her, or try to forbid her from going anywhere near it!

'Yes,' he admitted drily, his voice hardening, 'we've talked of ourselves and I've kissed you, all of which confirms my former suspicions that the sooner I dispose of Bilton Manor and leave the district, the better.'

Stacy flushed at his brutal frankness, while a strange twinge of hurt prompted her to return, with spirit, 'If you go so soon you can't expect us to miss you.'

He ignored this, with the contempt he obviously thought it deserved. 'What exactly has Paula been telling you?'

'Not much.'

With an exasperated sigh he reached for her again, holding her easily, so she got the feeling he liked being near her, although he might deny it. The hand which grasped her chin, however, was another thing. As he forced her face up it hurt. 'Come off it, Miss Weldon! You don't have to be devious, or tactfully discreet. Long ago I learnt how a woman is capable of discussing even the most intimate details of her life with a complete stranger.'

Stacy flinched at that, but it was, she reminded herself, exactly what she was. No feeling of having known this man from the beginning of time could alter the true facts. 'Maybe it's because often no one else will listen,' she snapped, 'but I don't think your mother went as far as that!'

'All right, calm down, Stacy Weldon,' he held up a cautionary hand before her small pink face. 'God knows, I'm a busy man, but I seem to remember doing my share of listening in the past.' He had the appearance of a man slightly driven, beyond even the limits of his enormous vitality, 'I'm only going to ask you once more, my child. What did she say to you?'

Apprehensively, Stacy felt compelled to answer, though she tried hard to be diplomatic, 'Just—just that she'd been left Bilton Manor, and ...'

'And?'

'And you don't really want her to live there.'

'No, I do not!'

'I can't really see, considering everything,' said Stacy, completely forgetting how she had denied being told anything, 'why you should object.'

His nostrils flared with impatience as his mouth clamped. 'I suppose she's been telling you I don't need her any more?'

'Well,' Stacy could have flayed herself for ever mentioning it, 'she—she did hint.'

'Hint!' he said grimly. 'Ever since I've been able to walk she's become more and more convinced. It's become a kind of obsession.'

'So she only wants to live here, on the other side of the world, to prove you still do need her?'

'No, Miss Weldon, that's where you're so wrong! She's coming to live here so she can believe I'm missing her like hell, but that I'm too far away to be able to do anything about it.'

It all seemed a bit too complex for Stacy, and she didn't feel intelligent enough to work it out, not then. 'I suppose what you're trying to say is that you really do need her after all?'

'No, Miss Weldon,' he said firmly, making her feel incredibly young and foolish, 'I do not need anyone, but I know how much my family need me. This is why, for her own good, mind you, I don't want you encouraging my mother to live here. And just think about it! She knows she can't manage alone. This is why, almost before she's set foot in the country, she's desperate to enlist someone's aid.'

'I still think it might be what she truly wants.'

'Allow me to be the best judge of that, Miss Weldon.'

'But your mother was born here, she lived here until she was married. Surely that counts for a lot?'

'Not after all this time.'

'Wouldn't you want to go back to your home,' Stacy cried, 'if ever you had to leave it?'

'I'm not a fool,' he gritted, 'but this situation is quite different.'

'She—' Stacy took one of the deep breaths which were coming to be a necessary ingredient in any conversation with Sloan Maddison. 'Your mother thinks you might be considering getting married, and your wife might not want her.'

'My God! How much more has she told you!'

It took all Stacy's courage to face his dark anger, especially when, for some reason she couldn't fathom, she felt depressed to even think of him with another woman. 'Well, if you intend getting married you can't be as self-sufficient as you try to make out.'

'Miss Weldon!' His black eyes were brilliantly taunting, 'I don't have to account to you. I don't have to answer your impertinent questions.'

She swallowed again. 'You're evading the issue.'

'I am?' A little light in his eyes seemed to flicker, as his gaze went mockingly over her. 'I didn't say I objected to having a woman to go to bed with, nor to marrying to provide myself with a necessary heir, but my mother doesn't have to leave Australia because of that. She could have a nice little establishment, anywhere she cares to choose in Queensland. Queensland alone has a land area over seven times the size of Britain, and from Brisbane, the capital, right up to Cape York in the north, there are any number of places she could happily settle. Some of her best friends live on the islands of the Barrier Reef, places she's always loved. She could even go and live beside my sister in Sydney. Sally would love to have her nearer.'

If he had looked even slightly harassed Stacy might have felt midly sympathetic, but his dark imperturbability, especially about having women in his bed—and their obvious uses—made her point out with acid relish, 'It seems, Mr Maddison, this is one problem which is going to prove too big for you.'

'Don't forget what I said about putting you over my knee,' he warned repressively. 'Do I have your promise to stay away from Bilton Manor?'

'I've already promised to go.'

'Well, back out.'

'I can't.'

'You mean you won't? You're just as stubborn and irresponsible as the rest of your sex. I think there's only one way to deal with a girl like you, even though I've known you only a few hours.'

He advanced, and Stacy retreated, caring nothing for the smouldering darkness in his eyes, the way they rested on her mouth, then flipped over her figure. She came up against the kitchen stove and, with determination, his hands were reaching for her when there came the sound of Mrs Weldon's car in the yard outside.

'Saved,' he muttered, without removing his eyes from Stacy's relieved face. 'Or was it simply prayers answered?'

'Mum does have to come home!' she pointed out.

'This I realise,' he responded drily, 'but we still have things to discuss.'

'I can't think of anything.' Stacy's voice was jerky, because Sloan Maddison didn't discuss things with her. He merely pointed out what she must do and hinted at the consequences of disobedience.

'Run along to bed,' he said, a faint curve to his mouth, which she couldn't exactly define. 'I want to speak to your mother.'

'Yes,' she agreed, glad to escape him. It wasn't until she was in her room that she became suddenly aware of how, in only a few hours, he had them all, including Betty, jumping to his every word of command!

The next morning she sat behind him as he drove Mrs Maddison and herself to Bilton Manor. They left Thorn Farm early as an architect had arranged to meet them, and was coming straight there from his home before going to his office in Birmingham.

Stacy had been up early, but there had been little to do. June, jealous of her position in the kitchen, never allowed her to do much, and Betty had been there almost with the milk. When Stacy had protested despairingly that it seemed slightly ridiculous, four women looking after two guests, Mrs Weldon had replied firmly that if she didn't advertise as a proper guesthouse it might have been. As it was she had a certain standard to keep up.

What was the use, Stacy thought, of trying to prove herself indispensable in a household clearly geared to managing without her? Nor had she realised how humiliating it could be to be considered an idle hanger-on. Not that anyone actually said so, in as many words, but this must surely be what they were all thinking.

When she had asked her mother what Sloan Maddison had wanted to speak to her about the previous evening, Mrs Weldon had merely replied that there had been several things he had been anxious to confirm regarding the immediate district, but nothing she had time to go into just then. Yet she had seemed to have plenty of time to elaborate on what a charming man he was, and it soon became very apparent to Stacy that her mother had greatly enjoyed her tête-à-tête at midnight.

It had been little comfort to know that because her mother had told her to be sure to be ready on time for her trip to Bilton Manor, Sloan Maddison could not have mentioned that he would rather Stacy stayed at home. If he had, Stacy was certain her mother would have produced some excuse to keep her from going.

The car was powerful, eating up the few miles between Thorn Farm and Bilton Manor in almost as many minutes. Sloan Maddison, she noticed, drove swiftly but carefully, as though the short, twisting roads of the rural English countryside were not altogether unknown to him.

The morning was bright but cold, and Stacy saw he wore a fine wool sweater under his jacket, belted trousers of a similar superb quality, and his hard, handsome looks made the breath tremble in her throat. Carefully she studied the back of his head, noting the slightly arrogant set of it on his broad shoulders, seeing the way in which his thick dark hair curled a little, in spite of being well brushed, against the firm brownness of his skin.

Suddenly, catching his eye in the driving mirror, she felt a thrill of something unnameable rush through her, and it took a great effort to turn away her silken head to look through the window. There had been no friendliness in his close regard and she knew he was angry that she was with them. Illogically it came to her that he hadn't mentioned their argument over her coming to Mrs Weldon, having decided to leave it to Stacy's good sense. That Stacy hadn't shown any was causing him no little displeasure, she could tell.

The Manor was approached by a long drive, but through neglect and lack of regular use was almost overgrown with grass. Neither this nor the house, which had been closed up for years, was looking its best. A previous housekeeper and her husband had been keeping an eye on it, but as they hadn't been paid anything they had done no more than check occasionally that it hadn't been broken into. Perhaps the nearby proximity of a farmhouse, which had once been the home farm, had done more to prevent this happening than anything else. A firm of builders had been employed to keep the roof in good order, but apart from this no other maintenance had been carried out.

It was a large house and well proportioned, but inside ceilings were down in some of the rooms and damp had damaged most of the furnishings beyond redemption. It soon became quite clear that, although it was structurally sound, Mrs Maddison would have to allow some time for the necessary repairs. As Stacy followed her from room to room, the prospect became more and more depressing.

The architect left, after a brief but comprehensive survey. Sloan Maddison had shown him around, his face grim but otherwise non-committal. After the surveyor's report, the architect assured Mrs Maddison that he would return again for a closer assessment before drawing up plans for her proposed alterations. Before leaving, he told them that he suspected dry rot in the main staircase, and advised them to use the old stone one which led from the kitchen.

Mrs Maddison, on hearing this, and probably fearing the dry rot had travelled further, firmly declined to venture upstairs but asked Sloan if he would go with Stacy, while she waited outside.

Stacy, who felt, in spite of a growing enthusiasm, that

she had had about enough of dust and cobwebs for one day, had to agree. The coldly challenging glance Sloan Maddison threw at her seemed to leave her with no alternative. The musty smell was making her feel slightly queasy, but pride would allow no retreat at this stage. She had an uneasy suspicion he was just waiting for her to give up.

'Don't worry,' he advised sardonically, while manipulating her carefully through the plaster-littered kitchen, 'I'm sure your admirable fervour for helping elderly ladies will make you oblivious to anything as mundane as dry rot.'

The back stairs, which led to what had once been the maids' bedrooms, were just as dirty as the rest of the house and Stacy was glad she was wearing her old blue jeans and a washable sweater, which couldn't really take much harm. It saddened her to see what could happen to even the nicest of old houses after a period of neglect.

'Now, Miss Weldon,' Sloan Maddison asked smoothly, as they wandered from one dusty room to another, 'how would you propose dealing with all this?'

Stacy viewed the collapsed ceilings he indicated despondently. 'I'm not a builder,' she protested, 'so that wouldn't be my problem. As for the decorating, I would have to have a little time to see the house as a whole, to sort of get the feel of it, but as far as I can see the rooms are nicely proportioned and wouldn't appear to present any unsurmountable difficulties.'

'You don't think,' his black brows rose as his sceptical glance roved the large proportions, 'it might be rather too big for one lone woman, and I'm talking about my mother.'

Stubbornly Stacy shook her silky head. She, too, was thinking of his mother. 'She could spend the rest of her life doing it up, restoring it to its former glory, so to speak. It could certainly give her a renewed interest in life.'

'And what then?'

'Well, she could always leave it to an institution or something, as,' with a sharp glance at her companion, 'no one else appears to want it.'

Reflectively, Sloan Maddison nodded. 'But she couldn't manage this herself.'

'I shouldn't think so,' Stacy pushed open another door and stood surveying the curtains of gauzy cobwebs which draped the bed and furniture in a ghostly white shroud. 'It might even be too much for a much younger woman to tackle on her own.'

'Just what I was thinking,' he agreed blandly.

A huge spider fell off the ceiling, disturbed by the invasion of his private domain. Repulsed, Stacy started back, and bumped up against Sloan Maddison, whose hands came out automatically to steady her. For one heart-stopping moment she rested against him, then she could feel her heart beating jerkily again beneath the blue sweater.

Her eyes wide with revulsion, she was barely conscious of him as she watched the mammoth spider slither clumsily to the faded carpet through the thick cobwebs. She was scarcely aware of Sloan pulling her closer to his hard, male body, until his hands slid under her sweater to find her taut breasts.

If she had been given any warning, she might have been able to have done something to prevent it, but the weakness which attacked her was too sweeping. Unable to move, she closed her eyes helplessly, becoming virtually a prisoner under the movement of his experienced fingers. Breathing fast, she felt one of his hands go to her waist, still holding her ruthlessly, while his other brushed the long loose hair from her nape, to enable his mouth to descend there. She could feel the insistent pressure on her soft skin, then his teeth.

She felt his hand pressing her head forward as the room began to spin and the now familiar heat began tearing through her slight body. Shuddering, from spinning senses, she tried to turn, so he could take her fully in his arms, but suddenly he was away from her, drawing her firmly from the room and closing the door. The shocked disbelief in her eyes as she stared at him, he obviously decided to put down to the spider.

'For a girl who's interested in this sort of thing, a dislike of spiders could be a distinct disadvantage,' he taunted, his eyes narrowed deviously. 'Had enough?'

If there was a double meaning to his question she didn't dwell on it. She felt horrified enough with her own immediate reactions without going any further. Every bit of her seemed to be burning with shame. She had a bra on and he had made no attempt to remove it. If she could forget how flimsy it was she might feel better.

'I asked,' he repeated, removing a long strand of her hair from his jacket, 'if you've seen enough.'

'Enough to get a general picture,' she mumbled.

'Remarkable, for one so blind in other ways,' he returned bitingly, his manner more distant than the hand he kept on her arm. As she tried to draw away from him, repelled by the coolness of his voice after the ardour of his mouth, he said crisply, 'I'm keeping a hold of you until we get down again, otherwise you might see another spider and take off from the top of the stairs. And this time I might not be in the right position to provide an antidote for your fright.'

So that was all it had been? Mutinously Stacy stared straight ahead. It seemed crazy to recall her crazy urge to cling to this man, but always it was there, whenever he kissed her. It was totally unbelievable, considering the shortness of their acquaintance, yet there was no denying she found Sloan Maddison attractive, in a way no other man had appealed to her. This tall cattleman, or station owner, or whatever he was called, could be dangerous to her peace of mind if she wasn't careful. In future she must take care not to be alone with him. The sooner he realised she wasn't here to provide some light entertainment while he was in Britain, the better.

Out in the pale March sunshine she found Paula leaning over a fence on the other side of the drive beyond where the car was parked, looking over the field which lay between the manor and the farmhouse.

'This must be the field on my deeds,' she exclaimed, as Stacy approached alone, having left Sloan busy locking up.

'It seems quite a large one.' Stacy saw it stretched some distance before a row of trees cut it off from the road on the other side.

'Yes,' Mrs Maddison continued, gazing over the field with complete satisfaction, 'it does, doesn't it? And there are, I've discovered, some stables around the back. I might have to buy in some fodder, but I'm sure I could easily keep two horses. I've always enjoyed riding.'

'Oh, so do I!' Stacy exclaimed, without thinking. 'I have to rely on the local stables, of course, or being able to borrow a horse.'

'Why not come and work for me, then, and we could go riding together? No need to borrow any more.' Mrs Maddison turned to Stacy happily.

'Work for you?'

'That's what I said. The house is so large I could never manage to restore it alone, but I like it, don't you? It's very different, I know, from Taronda, but I expect I shall soon get used to it.'

Stacy felt too startled to reply immediately. Instinctively she knew Sloan Maddison would want her to refuse. To say yes would amount to actively supporting his mother against him in encouraging her to stay here. Mrs Maddison, though, seemed determined to stay, regardless of anyone else's opinion, and if Stacy refused to work for her she would only offer the job to someone else. And it suddenly came to Stacy that she would rather work, now, for a woman than a man. If she worked for Mrs Maddison there would be no risk of meeting another Basil Bradley. As for Sloan Maddison, wasn't it unlikely that she would ever see him again after the next few days, whether his mother stayed here or not? Mrs Maddison would revisit Queensland alone, and Sloan had already stated he would be much too busy ever to return to Bilton Manor.

Paula Maddison was smiling, adding persuasively, throwing out her hands, 'My dear girl, you could have a free hand. Within reason you could decorate each room as you liked, and I promise I wouldn't be too demanding. You'd have plenty of spare time, and free horse riding, of course. I might even install a swimming pool, once we get the rest under way.'

Stacy, caught by Mrs Maddison's new animation, smiled at her warmly, 'I find myself too tempted to refuse!' A slight sound on the grass behind warned her, but too late. Swinging around, she caught the full blast of contemptuous anger in Sloan Maddison's black eyes.

'I scarcely think you need to bribe Miss Weldon further, Paula,' he said tightly, taking Stacy's arm and almost throwing her back into the car. 'If you keep on as you're doing you might soon not be in a position to afford her.'

All the way back to Thorn Farm Stacy was aware, through the stony silence, of things left unsaid, of a situation which appeared to be growing worse instead of better but which she didn't know how to improve. She didn't appreciate being manhandled by Sloan Maddison—resentfully she rubbed the bruises on her arm where his long, steely fingers had gripped—but she didn't really want to quarrel with him. Time was too short and she confessed, although she wouldn't openly admit it, that she would rather be in his arms, pursuing the peculiar excitement she found there. After Basil Bradley she had never thought she would want to be near another man again, yet she was beginning to think of Sloan Maddison almost continually.

Trying to dismiss this as nonsense, she wondered why he should attract her in any way at all. Previously she had always been too absorbed in her career to think of any man seriously. Certainly she had never been in love, but she knew wryly that this new sensation she felt in Sloan Maddison's arms wasn't that. It was merely some chemical reaction between them, a commonly acknowledged possibility between a man and woman, and Stacy felt ashamed, after his rough treatment of her, of the urge within her to feel his mouth on hers again. In that cobweb-shrouded room in the house they were leaving so rapidly behind, she had felt the quick passion in him, but he hadn't actually kissed her lips. Before this could happen he had thrust her away, and she supposed the fire she had imagined between them could have been the result of being taken by surprise. That he had been sufficiently in control of his emotions to call a halt proved his experience to be vastly greater than her own!

Again she found herself studying the back of his dark head, as she had done on their way to the Manor, and again she flushed on meeting his narrowed eyes in the driving mirror. This time the animosity she read there convinced her she would get no further opportunity of pursuing any kind of relationship with him, other than one based on his growing dislike. Thus stiffened, she resolved that she certainly wouldn't budge from her decision to work for his mother.

Lunch followed closely on their return to Thorn Farm, and the remainder of the day passed peacefully enough, with Sloan Maddison making a lightning visit to London and Mrs Maddison happily discussing her plans for Bilton Manor.

Paula, as soon as Sloan left, lost no time in informing Mrs Weldon that Stacy had agreed to work for her, and, from that day on, Stacy could consider herself employed. It would, of course, be quite a while before the Manor was ready for occupation, but she wanted to make sure of Stacy's services. Stacy again confirmed her willingness, and Mrs Weldon, delighted that Stacy was coming out of her long depression at last, expressed nothing but the utmost satisfaction. They celebrated with a glass each of a very good sherry, then Mrs Weldon insisted on taking Paula out to show her the village and one or two of the more famous beauty spots in the area before tea.

They had all retired to bed before Sloan Maddison came in, but no one worried as Mrs Weldon had given him a key. The first Stacy knew of his return was on being brought rudely awake, to find him sitting on the edge of her bed, shaking her.

'Shhh!'

'You?' She looked up quivering, jerking with sudden fright from his arousing hands, at the same time automatically trying to cover herself a little. It wasn't that she had nothing on—if Stacy indulged in one extravagance, it was that of having something glamorous to go to bed in. The nightdress she wore now was of a pale aquamarine satin, quite demure, apart from the narrow insets of toning lace on the bodice. Through this her young skin gleamed lustrously, and the burnished gloss of long hair, tumbling heavily over her bare shoulders, gave her the enticing look of a very young, pagan goddess. 'What are you doing here?' she cried, as momentarily he didn't speak. 'How did you know this was my bedroom, anyway?'

'Just by keeping my eyes open,' he rejoined tersely, removing his glance from her nightgown back to her startled young face. 'You don't have to squirm as though I'm here to attack your virtue. I might,' he added curtly, 'be having to use some restraint, but that wasn't my intention, and I have no wish to arouse the household.'

Yet he didn't go on, not right away. He had on a short dressing gown and his legs were bare, which made Stacy wonder if he wore anything underneath. He sat studying her, his eyes hooded, enigmatical, and feeling suddenly she might well be naked, she tried again to find the sheet. Of course Sloan had to be sitting on it, but when she asked him to move he made no effort. Leaning forward, she was opening her mouth to tell him exactly where he could go when his arms went around her, dragging her closer, his mouth coming down on her parted lips hard.

Yet the kiss, more intimate, Stacy thought wildly, than any kiss had a right to be, was shortlived. One moment he seemed about to devour her, the next he was pushing her brusquely back against her pillows. 'Don't tempt me, Stacy,' he said bluntly, 'I came here to talk, not make love.'

Half desperately, Stacy pushed back the tumbled mass of her hair from off her hot face, with fingers which trembled. She hoped he would put it down to the abruptness of her awakening, but somehow she doubted if he would. Her shoulders slumped as she realised how easily he could sum her up. In his arms she could scarcely hide a feverish response, though a second ago he had barely given her a chance of responding at all. All she could recall was the beginnings of an intimate exploration, then nothing. As coldly as she could she said flatly, 'You said that last night, and you talked enough then. I can't think what more you can want to speak to me about.'

'Can't you?'

'No.'

'I didn't deliberately invade your bedroom,' he said drily. 'I tried to get back earlier, but I happened to get delayed.'

'Really?'

'Stacy!' Even in the subdued glow of the bedside light he had switched on, she could see Sloan looked tired. The lines which were usually faint on his brow ran deep, and tonight there were also some around his mouth. She had an absurd longing to pull his head down beside her and comfort him with soft, tender kisses. It really seemed to hurt, seeing him so unusually vulnerable.

'Stacy!' There was nothing vulnerable in the way he repeated her name. His face was implacable and she felt herself shake at the grim tone of his voice. 'For heaven's sake, girl, stop sitting there pretending you don't know!'

She looked at him helplessly. 'It's because I promised to work for your mother?'

'And you're going to oblige me by changing your mind.' His eyes glittered over her, suddenly without their usual detachment, and his hand came out to touch her cheek. 'If it's only a job you're after, why not come back to Queensland with me? I could easily find you something there.'

'No, thank you!' Sharply she moved her head, shades of Basil Bradley looming in the shadows again. 'I can do without that kind of proposition, Mr Maddison.'

'Quit the Mr,' he commanded wearily. 'You and I seem to have come too far for such formality. Make it Sloan. And how was I to know you wouldn't jump at the chance?'

'You mean you aren't sure what sort of a girl I am?'

'Damn it, Stacy, the most innocent-looking packages often contain that which is far from innocent. How can a man tell before he takes a girl to bed?'

'You're probably right,' Stacy's heart beat with a strange kind of despondence. 'But there's such a thing as trust—and appearances. And common decency.'

Harshly he said, 'I don't think I've met a virgin yet.'

'Is that something you're proud of, Mr Maddison?' she asked furiously.

'You haven't answered my question about changing your mind,' he reminded her, ignoring the one she had put to him.

Her mind diverted quite nimbly, seeing how he'd almost struck her dumb, 'Haven't you ever thought, Sloan Maddison, if I don't take this job with your mother she will only offer it to someone else?'

'Maybe,' his teeth drew back, 'but it's from you she's getting the courage to stay. Oh, I agree, she's in love with the idea of it all, but before coming to Thorn Farm she had plenty of niggling apprehension. I'm just beginning to realise the stupidity of staying here. If we'd gone to a large luxury hotel, where she hadn't got to know anyone, she'd have put Bilton Manor in the hands of an estate agent and been on her way home by now. As it is, she sees in you and your family some kind of definite insurance against ever being alone in a country which is now unfamiliar to her. She and your mother obviously like each other, and she's settling in as though she's lived here all her life. Only if you refuse to work for her might I persuade her to change her mind.'

'No, never!' Stacy stared at him, wondering why she had to be so emphatic, why there was such a need in her to fight this man. She wasn't really fighting him, she knew, about his mother, but a battle won might make her stronger to face another.

'You really mean that, don't you?'

'I ... Yes, I do.'

'Do you realise,' he said harshly, 'I could make you change your mind, if I really wanted to?'

'How?'

His eyes flashed as he retaliated grimly, 'I've held you in my arms. I can feel how you react—— You aren't exactly frigid, Stacy Weldon, though I don't think you've had much experience.'

Her heart beat and her cheeks burned, and her eyes were glued to the broad, rugged strength of his dark chest. 'What does that prove?' she whispered.

'That you might be quite willing to do as I ask, if I stayed with you until daylight.'

Her eyes widened as feeling tore jaggedly through her, hurting, burning her right up. 'No! I won't listen,' she cried breathlessly, clasping both hands over her ears.

'So you won't change your mind?' He grasped her tightly, his fingers cruel, forcing her to drop her hands in an effort to push him away.

'You can be sure I won't.' Because of her fright, she

twisted frantically in his arms, but just as she felt the menace of his breath on her face he let her go.

'You wouldn't be worth the trouble,' he ground out, heaping insult on injury, as his hands left their mark, this time on the tender skin of her shoulders.

He rose from the bed, but before leaving her he said heavily, 'I don't know what you hope to gain by this, other than a comfortable life, which I shouldn't have thought would be of paramount importance at your age. But you've apparently made up your mind and I won't keep on trying to make you change it. Just one thing I will say. You've chosen to be employed by my mother, so don't ever let me hear of you cheating her in any way, or of letting her down. If you do, even if I have to come all the way from Australia, I'll come back and wring your charming little neck!'

CHAPTER FOUR

THE almost sleepless night which followed Sloan Maddison's abrupt departure from Stacy's bedroom didn't help her appearance next morning, but Mrs Maddison was still too full of excitement over Bilton Manor to notice anything amiss. Stacy's apathy actually suited her as it did nothing to interrupt the full flow of her enthusiasm.

Sloan Maddison went out again soon after breakfast, and Stacy suspected he was looking into his mother's business more closely than she suspected. Obviously he would be trying to prove the house was a white elephant. Stacy avoided him by staying in the kitchen until he had gone, but Betty's running commentary on his 'smashing good looks' hadn't helped.

Stacy felt so shaken that morning she didn't hear very much of what Paula Maddison was saying, but when she realised this she was ashamed and made a greater attempt to pull herself together. What was the good of feeling bitter because Sloan had proved quite clearly that his brief, though potent, kisses had been distributed only in an effort to prevent her from agreeing to work for his mother, but while she didn't think, now, he would continue trying to make her change her mind, the warning he had issued seemed just as unnerving.

Mrs Maddison, that morning, was overflowing with plans. 'I shall stay here. You can consider yourself fully employed from this moment.' Her eyes sparkled with enthusiasm as she smiled at Stacy.

Biting her lip doubtfully, Stacy consented, but felt forced to point out that it could be some months before the house was ready for occupation. 'Won't you be going back to

Australia with—with Mr Maddison for a while?'

'No,' replied Paula, though at the mention of Australia she paused uncertainly. 'I'll admit I did think of it, but I'm not so sure any more. I don't think I will go back, if I don't have to, and I'll get the solicitor whom I've employed over here to sort out the various formalities. No,' she went on, 'there's plenty we can be getting on with, in spite of the house not being ready. We can measure a few of the rooms and look at furniture, for instance, and you could make a start on working out the decor for the rooms we'll occupy as soon as the worst of the dust and dirt has been cleared. I imagine a firm of proper cleaners will be best for this, and then there'll be staff to employ. No one's apparently willing to come at a moment's notice these days, at least not the kind of staff I have in mind. I'm afraid you'll have to be prepared to act as my secretary for a while. I want to begin looking up my scattered relations as soon as possible and, as I can't drive, you'll have to take me around. No, my dear, I don't think you need worry about having nothing to do.'

Stacy wasn't sure why she should point out, as Mrs Maddison paused for breath, 'Mr Maddison still doesn't seem very keen about you living at the Manor.'

'No, I suppose not.' Paula glanced at Stacy with a small hint of satisfaction, which somehow seemed to bear out what Sloan had said. 'I'm afraid he's going to miss me more than he realises, but he must discover he can't always have everything his own way.'

Mrs Maddison was to prove indefatigable over her new home. She kept Stacy busy all day. After numerous phone calls and various pieces of correspondence had been dealt with, she ordered a taxi to take them to Birmingham for shopping, and to bring them home again via Bilton Manor. There she apprehended the surveyor in the middle of his work, proceeding to follow him around and over various obstacles, in a way Stacy wasn't sure was fit for a middle-aged woman. She felt as relieved as the surveyor looked when Paula decided to call it a day and left.

Later Stacy felt so exhausted, if it hadn't been Richard's birthday she might well have refused to attend the small celebration party which June had secretly planned for him.

'It's only supper and a cabaret with a few friends,' June explained, naming the latter, so there was no one Stacy knew she could object to, even had she wanted to, 'and a birthday is a rather special occasion.'

With dinner over, June wouldn't take no for an answer. Dragging Stacy upstairs, she ordered her to put on something glamorous, for a change. 'Find that blue dress you bought in London,' she said, 'the one you've never had the courage to wear. I'm almost ready myself, but I'll give you ten minutes. Richard's due any time, so don't keep us waiting.'

Feeling suddenly infected, in spite of her weariness, by June's cheerfulness, Stacy hurried as fast as she could. After a quick shower she splashed on body lotion extravagantly, then slid into the blue silk. It was a beautiful dress and it suited her, but it was one she had bought on impulse and, at the front, the neckline dipped almost to the waist. It was the first time she had ever worn an evening dress without a bra, and although nearly every girl tonight would be wearing something similar, Stacy wondered if she had the necessary confidence to carry it off. She didn't want to spend the evening feeling embarrassed as well as tired.

It was just to please her sister, and because the nightclub they were going to was smart and sophisticated, that she decided to keep it on. Apart from June and Richard and their two or three friends, no one else would know her and her old fur cape, from her schooldays, would keep her covered until she got there. Stooping, she thrust her feet into high-heeled silver sandals, then picking up her bag she ran downstairs, her long, shining hair floating out behind her.

In the hall she was startled to find June chatting gaily

with Richard and Sloan Maddison. Both men wore dark jackets and ties, both were tall, but there the resemblance ended. Sloan Maddison, for all he was supposed to spend most of his time in the Never-Never, appeared the much more polished of the two. His air of easy command was unmistakable yet his black eyes, momentarily softening at something June was saying, betrayed an undeniable sensitivity, and when he replied Stacy was struck afresh by his very attractive voice. Richard was younger, a rather serious, extremely earnest young man who always acted with the best of intentions. Being almost one of the family, as he and June were to be married in a few months' time, he knew about Stacy's unfortunate encounter with Basil Bradley. After it had happened he had had to be almost forcibly restrained from going to confront Basil in person.

Stacy, not having seen Sloan all day, felt her cheeks colour with what she refused to believe as guilt, as he turned to look at her. Miserably she lowered her own eyes, never finding it easy to meet his with any convincing equanimity.

June spotted her with evident relief, 'Ah,' she cried, 'so you're ready at last!' as if they had been waiting hours instead of minutes. 'Sloan is coming, too,' she smiled, much to Stacy's consternation, consternation which changed to a baffling kind of depression as June added teasingly, 'I want to give some of the girls a treat.'

Frowning, Stacy wondered why this didn't altogether appeal to her, while Sloan obviously put down her changed expression to something else. As they left, he caught her arm. 'You don't have to look so put out because I'm coming with you. I won't continue to pester you about working for Paula, if that's what you're worrying about. I've said all I'm going to say.'

But he didn't say he would take any of it back! Nervously she stood biting her lip as June, taking charge as usual, arranged how they should travel.

'Would you mind taking Stacy with you, Sloan?' she

asked. 'You see, I promised to pick up some friends and Richard's car wouldn't be big enough to accommodate the lot of us.'

Sloan nodded, apparently not noticing the angry glance Stacy threw at her sister. Like Richard, he seemed to understand and appreciate June's nice touch of authority. Despairingly she regarded June's calm efficiency, which could make life run as smooth as clockwork. The mess she had made of her own life surely didn't bear comparison!

As she could offer no reasonable excuse of objecting, she made her way to Sloan's car. 'It's too big,' she muttered as, after closing her door, he got in beside her.

'Too big?' he flicked the ignition. 'What for?'

'Well,' she almost stammered, as his arm touched hers, 'Considering the price of gas.'

'Oh, I see.'

He sounded so uninterested she squirmed, and sank, with a quiver of humiliation and resentment, into her corner. She wanted to sit and say nothing, to refuse to answer his next comment, but his own cold silence robbed her of even this small triumph.

At last, tried beyond endurance, she was provoked to speak. 'You couldn't really want to come out with us tonight. I'm sure June wouldn't have minded if you'd refused.'

'I rarely do anything I don't want to,' he retorted bluntly, 'as I believe I've told you before. When you know me better you'll realise.'

If his choice of words struck her as peculiar, she didn't dwell on them. 'I'm sorry,' she murmured, too sharply for any graciousness to show through. 'I just thought you might not want to hurt June. It might be considered we're stepping a bit out of line, even to ask you. After all, you're a guest, and a pretty affluent one at that.'

'I'm certainly going to accuse you of stepping out of line if you go on like this,' he said curtly, turning quietly out on to the main road, following Richard's disappearing tail lights. 'It might be a good idea to forget you don't like me for the next few hours, otherwise you could risk spoiling your sister's party.'

'I suppose so,' whispered Stacy, feeling suddenly near to unpredictable tears. 'She and Richard love each other.'

'How long have they been engaged?'

'A few months.'

'That's one thing I don't believe in.' He turned his head to glance at her and she quivered at something in his expression.

'What don't you believe in?' she gulped.

'Long engagements. I wouldn't have the patience, not if I'd got as far as deciding to marry.'

Her stomach churning, which must be because she had eaten so little dinner, Stacy breathed, 'You wouldn't give her a chance to change her mind?'

'She wouldn't want to,' his voice was full of a dark confidence, 'not once she belonged to me.'

The journey into Birmingham was over in a very short time. It was the second time Stacy had been there that day, and without thinking she said so.

'You were here with my mother. She mentioned it.'

'Yes.' She wished he'd sounded pleased.

'She also said you officially began working for her today.'

'Yes.'

'Dear me,' he mused, 'what a vocabulary!' Then, quite harshly, 'So you really don't intend taking any notice of my advice? I had hoped. However, before we begin our truce, Stacy Weldon, you will be sure to remember what I told you last night about letting her down?'

'I don't intend to,' she rejoined, hating him for reminding her of an interval she would rather forget. 'But I'm sure you'll make sure I won't,' she added bitterly, 'some way or another.'

He found the club in Birmingham with an ease which might have put a native to shame. Ten minutes later, having waited for June and Richard to join them after picking up their other guests, they were all seated inside.

The interior of the club, to which Stacy had been only twice before, was very plush with its velvet seating and pearly beige walls and thickly carpeted floors. Under the laser lights the girls' skins gleamed and their jewellery sparkled discreetly. Most of the girls, Stacy noticed, wore the same sort of fluttery, floating dress as herself with, if anything, even lower necklines. She needn't have worried about her own!

The floor show was good. One of the vocalists, a singer with a well known group, appeared to be putting everything she had into it. There was nothing reticent about her extravagant gesticulating, and she was very sexy. She wore one of the little-nothing dresses which cost a fortune and it emphasised every voluptuous curve of her figure. Stacy was sure she glanced more than once towards where Sloan sat watching enigmatically.

Even June noticed. 'Have you met her before, Sloan?' she asked, with an amused twinkle. 'These groups get around.'

Sloan gave a slight smile, 'I believe I have seen this one on the Gold Coast, which is near Brisbane. Near Surfers Paradise and other places you could find almost everything in the way of entertainment.' He turned to Stacy with a glance of mocking amusement. 'Some of the floor shows down there would make you blink—and blush, I'm afraid, though that's not to say that they're not usually beautifully presented and enjoyable.'

Sipping her champagne, which Sloan had insisted was necessary to toast Richard's birthday, Stacy marvelled at the way in which he seemed to fit in wherever he went. Not exactly unobtrusively, for he was a man who would always be noticed in a crowd, but he had a kind of worldly charisma about him which she doubted he had been born with, and which she was just as sure he hadn't acquired entirely on an Outback cattle station. Envy touched her unexpectedly, as she wondered what kind of girl had shared the delights of this Gold Coast with him.

June had picked up three friends, two girls and a man, and it occurred to Stacy that if she had refused to come the numbers would have been just right. As it was she felt very much the odd one out as one of the other girls, a vivacious blonde, almost demanded Sloan's attention.

The evening was almost over before he asked Stacy to dance. There wasn't much in the way of a floor and it was crowded. He held her close, but whether this was for his own pleasure or her protection, she didn't know.

'I like your dress,' he murmured, 'and your perfume,' and he bent his head appreciatively nearer.

'It was a present from Paris,' she said, still feeling too stiff from the resentment he had aroused by dancing nearly the entire evening with the other girls to mention that her mother had brought it.

'Didn't he take you with him?' Sloan mocked, immediately presuming it had been a man.

'I keep it for special occasions.' She decided not to enlighten him.

After a moment his face softened again, as if he had decided not to allow something to annoy him, not then. 'You always smell nice,' his tone suggested he had been close enough to discover, 'look nice, too.' He held her slightly from him, his eyes darkening as they slowly pursued the low line of her dress to where it revealed her figure as she swayed with him. His fingertips touched her long-chained necklace, his hand slipping under it to lift it for his closer inspection. 'You deserve better than this,' he smiled.

'It's not what I deserve,' she tried to speak flippantly, so as not to reveal how his hand, still lying against the warm skin of her breast was affecting her, 'but what I can afford.'

'The next time your friend goes to Paris tell him to bring you jewellery, perhaps a sapphire necklace to match your eyes.'

Stacy knew she should be retreating in anger, but she seemed suddenly beyond making any definite move. Sloan's arm was tight around her, pressing her up against the hardness of his thighs, in a way too intimate to resist. Feeling shivered through her, burning her, and she was sure he could feel her trembling through the thinness of her dress. She seemed to be floating, in a kind of trance, and her eyelids fell helplessly as she melted against him. Murmuring something, she tried to speak, but the deepening pressure of his hands swept away the last of her resistance. Slowly he lowered his head, turning it slightly until his lips touched her cheek. Then the music stopped.

'Short and sweet,' he said ruefully, but his eyes were watchful as he took her back to their table, and he kept a firm hand under her arm as though he guessed her limbs felt weak.

Not long afterwards they left, and for all Stacy heard the blonde girl blatantly begging Sloan to take her home, he must have refused as he went with Stacy.

'Did you enjoy yourself?' he asked, when they were within a few miles of Thorn Farm.

It was almost the first time he had spoken since they had left the city. He had seemed preoccupied, and she couldn't help wondering if he was regretting not having taken the other girl home. Or was he perhaps considering how he might contact her and arrange a date? Stacy acknowledged the feeling of envy this evoked with some dismay. It was just as well he was returning soon to Australia!

'Yes, thank you,' she replied, in a polite little voice, because she couldn't very well say anything else.

He laughed, although he didn't sound too amused, 'You sound very like a small girl after her first party! I don't think you enjoyed yourself all that much. In fact I'd go as far as to say I had a feeling something was worrying you.'

'Just as long as you don't believe you are,' she threw back in panic.

'I would like to believe I could,' he rejoined coolly, 'but you've already proved you couldn't care less about me.'

That wasn't true. Nervously Stacy bit her lip. She might have given this impression, but it wasn't true. Yet how could she tell him this? He was only here for a few more days and time was flying, but some things were too difficult to put into words. Nor would it be easy to find the right words to express her true feelings when she scarcely knew what they were herself. Inexplicably her breath caught on a sigh of frustration.

Sloan Maddison, alert to the slightest sound, caught it. 'What's that supposed to mean, regret or impatience?'

Her silky head fell back against the seat as uncertainty stormed through her. Something drove her to speak without her usual caution. 'The—the former, if anything.'

'About me?'

Her sigh came again, but it was fretful this time. She was finding it difficult to be devious at this hour of night, with her mind refusing to concentrate. Sloan was sitting beside her and she was too conscious of him. It was incredible how her mind clung to the very solid ghost of him sitting on her bed, and even more startling to realise she would rather he was there now, so they might both try to discover without words, exactly what she did mean.

Almost as if he could read her thoughts, his hand came to cover hers as it lay clenched on her lap. 'Stacy, don't I tempt you at all to want to get to know me better?'

It was such a change, after the coolness he had shown for most of the evening, that her heart did a kind of double flip, before settling to a running beat. She made a helpless little gesture with her shoulders. 'I—I wouldn't mind, but I couldn't go with you to Australia.'

'Forget I asked,' he said, after a brief silence, but he took his hand away.

Swallowing back what seemed surprisingly like a sob, she tried to speak carelessly. 'As you'll be gone in a few days, getting to know each other could be pointless.'

'Little fool!' His voice hardened, but with what she

wasn't sure. It could have been contempt, or determination. 'A lot has been achieved in less time than that—it depends how badly you want something. You denied it while I was there, but did you really want me to leave you last night, Stacy?'

Flinching as if stung, she drew back from him, but his hand whipped out again, this time to tighten like steel around her wrist, where she felt his thumb measuring the frantic beat of her pulse.

'I'm not sure,' she whispered, knowing her alarmed gasp might be nearer the truth than she supposed. While terror and curiosity urged her on, she knew she could never go as far as admit to a man that she wanted him. Perhaps it was easier after the first time, but some fastidious part of her wanted to keep that first experience for marriage. Yet what did a girl do when she suspected the only man she might ever want to marry could prove as inaccessible as the moon? If she could find the right kind of courage, wouldn't she be wiser to settle for a few days of stolen delight?

Sloan, on a stretch of straight road, released her wrist to put his arm round her, pulling her close, his hand sliding under her unbuttoned fur coat to find her breast. 'I haven't forgotten where your room is,' he said thickly.

Feeling almost sick with emotion, Stacy huddled against him, too unnerved to find the breath to protest. His hand moved to her waist, as though he didn't intend to over-persuade her, but she sensed he was still impatient for her answer.

It was a big step to take, she doubted if she could, yet the feeling which was growing inside her for this tall Australian seemed to be sweeping away all her old inhibitions. She could barely think straight and, uncertainly, she glanced up at him, knowing instinctively that he was a man who usually took what he wanted. But there was no love on his face. Lust might harden a man's face—she remembered how Basil Bradley's had been stamped with the same ruthless purpose—but love surely softened it. A chill ran through her, so that she shivered from the cold of it and turned away. It was quite obvious that whatever else Sloan felt for her it wasn't love.

The car stopped, she realised suddenly that they were home, and felt vaguely grateful that Sloan hadn't attempted to draw off the road in some dark lane and take her in his arms.

In the yard outside the house a light still burned. It fell full on Sloan's face as he switched off the engine and turned to look at her. 'Stacy?'

He had removed his arm from around her; he must have done so as they had turned into the drive, but she had been too full of indecision to notice. She was aware that her name was a prompt to the question he had put indirectly a few minutes ago, but she knew now she couldn't do what he seemed to be asking. 'I'm sorry, Sloan,' she stammered bleakly, 'I—I don't know what to say, but I can't...'

Unable to go on, she stared at him, her blue eyes wide with a kind of anguish, which might easily have betrayed her.

For a long moment he stared back at her, only the knuckles of one of his hands, as it gripped the steering wheel, indicating he might be fighting an impulse to make some physical movement. At last he said quietly, with no hint of anger, 'Don't worry, Stacy. Four days isn't long. I had no right, anyway, to ask this of a girl as young and innocent as you.'

Without another word he left the car, but before he could get around to her side she had released her door and stumbled out after him. A sense of inadequacy driving her, she wanted suddenly to put his needs before what seemed her own selfishness. 'Sloan!'

But he wasn't listening. He had turned to watch Mrs Weldon running frantically from the house, and as if suddenly realising she was distraught, strode forward to meet her.

'Oh, thank goodness you're back!' she cried, as Sloan reached her. A rough patch of gravel had her stumbling and he put a hand out to steady her.

'What's wrong, Mrs Weldon?' His curt tone seemed to calm her, making Stacy realise, even through her alarm, that in an emergency he might be a man in a million.

'Mum?' She had her mother's other arm, but Mrs Weldon was looking at Sloan.

'It's your mother, Sloan. She collapsed, about ten minutes ago. She's upstairs, and I've rung for a doctor, and an ambulance—I might have made a mistake, but I'm almost certain an ambulance is going to be needed. I've just been in touch with the club, but they said you'd left.'

'I see.' Sloan Maddison's face was expressionless, although Stacy noticed he had paled a little. 'It's cold out here for you,' he said, as Mrs Weldon shivered. 'We'd better get inside, then you can tell me exactly what happened.'

'What did happen, Mum?' Stacy asked apprehensively, as she followed them upstairs, feeling almost as shocked as her mother looked.

'It must have come on as she got into bed,' Mrs Weldon panted, glancing at Sloan. 'We'd spent a very pleasant evening watching TV and just talking. I don't think I'd been in my room for more than a few minutes when your mother rang.'

Sloan went straight to his mother's bedside, speaking to her quietly as she turned to him. Clasping his hand tightly, she was obviously in some pain, and when she began trying to pull herself up, as though she wanted to talk to him, he pushed her gently back, advising her to rest quietly until the doctor arrived.

'I can't think what can be wrong with me,' she gasped, 'It all happened so quickly. I feel terrible.'

'I know,' Sloan seemed intent on soothing her, 'but it might be nothing much.'

'Maybe not.'

'Have you any idea what caused it? Have you been feeling all right lately?'

Paula twisted her greying head feverishly. 'Perhaps I did too much at the Manor yesterday. I was just trying to show Stacy what I wanted done."

Stacy frowned, as she stood beside her mother, watching Sloan patting Paula's hand reassuringly. She couldn't recall this being the reason why Paula had insisted they went to Bilton after leaving Birmingham. At the time Mrs Maddison had said she couldn't wait to hear the surveyor's verdict, and that if she could waylay him he might be willing to give her some idea of the true condition of the house immediately. Stacy could only suppose she didn't want Sloan to know this and had trotted out the first excuse to come into her head. Judging from the darkness of the look he was casting in her direction, Stacy realised that it would be on her head his wrath would fall. Unable to meet the cold condemnation in his eyes, she looked away.

As the doctor arrived and Stacy heard her mother sigh with heartfelt relief, she turned and went to her own room. Slipping out of her dress and the long silky underskirt which went with it, she was busy searching for something more practical when the door opened and Sloan came in. Gasping, she tried to grab her dressing gown, but he took little notice of her near-nudity.

'You were going to bed?' his enquiry was coldly contemptuous, as his eyes went indifferently over her.

'No, I wasn't!' she hissed, turning her back to him as she dragged her robe over the bareness of her trembling body, and fastening the cord. Brushing back her long hair from pink cheeks, she turned to him again. 'I was only changing into something shorter.'

'You'd better be,' he snapped curtly. Then, 'Just what were you and Paula doing at the damned house this afternoon? You didn't tell me you'd been anywhere near it.'

Uncertainly, Stacy hesitated. It would feel too much like a betrayal to say that, far from encouraging Paula to visit Bilton that afternoon, she had tried to advise her against it, after their hectic round of the city shops.

'There didn't seem much harm in dropping in,' she said evasively, 'when we were passing.'

'I can't understand how you could be doing that,' he retorted tightly, 'when Bilton lies in the opposite direction.'

As she stared at him anxiously, Stacy's mind was too tired to find another excuse easily, but apparently he wasn't prepared to listen to any more.

'You're inventive but not very bright, unfortunately. We'll just have to hope you improve. Anyway, I can see that Paula will be going to hospital, and as you're employed by her, I think you'd better come with us. It surely won't be too great a strain, even for your intelligence, to sit with her in the ambulance.'

'Are you going?' asked Stacy.

'I'll follow in the car, which we might need, if only to return here. You didn't think I'd let her go alone, did you?'

'No!' Stacy felt so upset she had to cover it up with a glare. 'That wasn't what I meant at all. I just didn't think she'd want me, if you were to be there.'

'She's been asking for you, and she's paying you.' The hardness on his face dared her to utter another word.

'Of course I'll be glad to come.' She turned towards her wardrobe, unable to bear his harsh unfriendliness.

'Be ready,' he warned, leaving to retrace his steps to the sickroom.

The doctor diagnosed acute appendicitis, and Stacy went with Paula to the hospital in Birmingham. Mrs Weldon had wanted to accompany them, but Sloan refused to allow her. He could see she was almost exhausted and he didn't know when they would be back. Paula would probably be operated on right away, and the doctor saw no reason to suspect complications, but Sloan promised he would ring as soon as it was over.

Stacy, her heart full of compassion, held Paula's hand all the way. Paula was calmer, though still in a great deal of pain.

'You're a good child, Stacy,' she smiled weakly. 'It seems strange how I feel as though I'd known you—and your family—all my life. Your mother and I spent last night like old friends.'

Remembering what Sloan had had to say about that, Stacy swallowed, but Paula didn't seem to notice her discomfort.

'Is Sloan coming?' she asked.

'Yes. He's following.' Stacey didn't want to encourage Paula to talk too much. Perspiration beaded Paula's brow and Stacy wiped it away with a soft tissue.

Paula smiled her thanks. 'He's really very dependable, you know. At home no one moves without his say-so. He's very anxious to get back.' A moment's silence. 'I don't know what he's going to do about this!'

'Well, it can happen to anybody,' Stacy pointed out, and with an optimism she felt fully justified, added bitterly, 'I'm sure he'll think of something.'

'Barbara will be waiting for him,' Paula murmured drowsily. 'That's maybe half his hurry.'

Feeling herself growing strangely cold, Stacy gazed at Paula's white face. Mrs Maddison, she half suspected, was not entirely aware of what she was saying, but mightn't this not be all the more reason to believe she was speaking the truth? Naturally, in Sloan Maddison's life there would be women. While well aware of this, Stacy had kept such thoughts half hidden in her subconsciousness. To have to face it was oddly painful.

'Does—does Barbara love him?' she whispered.

'She wants him, anyway.' Paula grimaced, closing her eyes, so Stacy couldn't tell if she approved or not.

There followed some of the longest hours Stacy had ever spent. It wasn't that she was overcome with grief, she hadn't known Mrs Maddison long enough for that, but remorse kept hitting her because she felt she ought to have been able to have stopped Mrs Maddison romping around, like a two-year-old, at Bilton Manor. While Doctor Blanes hadn't said this could have aggravated Mrs Maddison's condition, Stacy couldn't help feeling guilty about it, and Sloan's cold face wasn't reassuring. He sat beside her in the waiting room like a stranger, and this, she supposed, unwilling to face the truth, was after only a few days what he still was.

He was as polite as one, too. He kept supplying her with cups of tea she didn't want and asking if she was comfortable. If his expression had only been a little warmer she wouldn't have cared if he'd never bothered with any of these things. Naturally he was worried, and his worries must appear to be multiplying, but surely he couldn't blame her for the whole of them? He talked occasionally to a nurse, who Stacy could see liked the look of him, but otherwise he had little to say.

It was daylight on a cold March morning before they were told Mrs Maddison was going to be all right. Sloan waited until she came around and spent a few minutes with her before driving Stacy home.

'You'd better try and get some sleep,' he said curtly. 'You look as though you could do with it.'

'Thanks,' she returned drily.

'Stacy!' In the dimness of the hall he reached out, pulling her to him, but the action was threatening rather than lover-like, as if he would liked to have crushed her against the hardness of his chest. 'I can do without your sarcasm this morning.' His eyes very near her own, were like flint.

'I'm sorry,' she breathed unevenly, her face curiously strained as she subdued an impulse to press comfortingly against him, to try and show him how truly sorry she was. 'Sloan,' she exclaimed, in a feverish rush, 'I know you're blaming me about your mother . . .'

'Leave it!' Abruptly he let her go, as if he felt the accelerating race of her heart. 'I happen to be tired myself.'

'I was only trying to explain, to prove how sorry I am.'

'Fine,' he said narrowly, watching her sway, like a finely drawn flower, shaken by weariness. 'There might be some way you can make amends, or doesn't this appeal to you?'

Feeling drawn to him powerfully, she whispered huskily, 'I'd do anything to—to make amends. I'm not naturally careless or uncaring. If there's anything, anything at all I can do for your mother, you have only to ask.'

'I'll most certainly keep that in mind.' His gaze was suddenly so ruthless she shivered.

It seemed very much like one of the many threats he had been issuing of late, but through her uneasiness Stacy saw the new lines of strain around his eyes and mouth. 'Aren't you going to get some rest?' she queried.

He smiled grimly. 'Missing a night's sleep is nothing unusual for me. A cup of coffee and I'll be as good as new. I have too much to see to to go to bed.'

'But your mother will be all right for a little while.'

'It's not that. I have to go to London, I'm afraid. I decided when I was over here to attend to some business of my own, and I've an appointment I don't want to break.'

'Oh, I see.'

His hand on her arm tightened. She hadn't been aware of him drawing her close again. 'Stacy——' he began, his voice suddenly changing. Then, as her mother came from the kitchen, obviously eager for fresh news, he let her go, with a low mutter of impatience. Yet not a hint of it showed, in either his face or manner, as he turned politely to speak to the woman coming quickly towards them.

CHAPTER FIVE

THE next few days seemed to be composed of a strange mixture of hours, those which crawled and a few that rushed by. Whenever Sloan was around, either when, together, they visited his mother, or dining alone afterwards, time appeared to fly on dazzling wings, but when he was out, as he usually was during the mornings and early afternoons, Stacy thought she could count every second in each long minute.

With a caution born from an unconscious desire to protect herself from hurt, she refused to think what it was going to be like when he returned to Australia, but when occasionally her thoughts fixed on this and refused to be diverted, she managed to convince herself it would simply be a case of out of sight, out of mind. Scornfully, if she ever doubted this, she would remind herself of Basil Bradley, and that it wasn't possible to recover from the shock he had given her so quickly. Whatever she felt for Sloan Maddison could be nothing more than a mild infatuation based on some kind of reaction, and hadn't he proved he might be no better than Basil Bradley if he got the chance?

She recalled how Sloan had been that first night in her bedroom, and didn't try to delude herself that he was anything less than a full-blooded man. Suspecting he wouldn't be satisfied with anything less than total commitment from a girl who really took his fancy, Stacy wondered with a shiver if this Barbara whom Mrs Maddison had mentioned allowed him to take liberties she hadn't. Perhaps, Stacy argued with herself, such a relationship might be excusable if a girl really loved a man, but to give in to a merely physical attraction could surely bring no lasting happiness?

Yet would Sloan be hurrying back to Barbara if he didn't love her? With his mother still in hospital, Stacy somehow doubted it. Only some stronger, different emotion would persuade him to leave his mother just now, and Stacy found herself shivering with an unhappiness which seemed strangely worse than anything she had previously known.

Each afternoon she went to visit Paula Maddison in hospital. Twice Mrs Weldon had gone with her, but usually she went alone. Sloan had made it clear from the beginning that she was to consider this part of her new job, the job Paula had engaged her for. When Stacy, feeling hurt because he had seemed to imagine she wouldn't visit Paula otherwise, had righteously declared she would do everything she could for his mother but wouldn't take any salary for it, he had countered immediately by asking if she was trying to take the easy way out. It was his ruthless insistence that she was to continue to regard herself as Paula's employee, even while his mother was scarcely capable of giving an order, which bewildered and puzzled Stacy.

Each afternoon she drove into Birmingham, spending a longer time with Paula, as she grew stronger, then she went home before returning in the evenings with Sloan. Afterwards she and Sloan dined in the city before going back to Thorn Farm. When Mrs Weldon protested that June could easily have a meal ready for him, he had insisted he couldn't face the return journey on an empty stomach and, because he was never quite sure what time they might leave the hospital, it could be food wasted.

Stacy, feeling guilty that she should argue with him about this, found herself looking forward too much to these intimate nightly meals to raise many objections. In a congenial mood, she soon discovered, Sloan Maddison, as a companion, couldn't be faulted, and when they kept off the more sensitive areas regarding themselves, they could talk. Occasionally she found herself surprised that they could talk to each other so easily, and several times she had been almost convinced Sloan found her conversation entertaining.

He drew her out to talk of her childhood on the farm, of her adored and sadly missed father. Sloan had mentioned how he had read an article of his in an international journal, and wished he had known him. Stacy, in turn, found what he had to tell her about Australia so interesting that she found herself watching him with a wistful feeling in her heart—a feeling which often mounted to despair as she realised it might never be possible for her to go there.

There was no doubt that Sloan enjoyed these dinners as much as she did and, if the ghost of the mysterious Barbara continued to haunt her, on these occasions at least Stacy managed to keep her firmly in the background. Telling herself it wasn't that she wanted to impress him but because it was part of her job, she tried to dress smartly. One afternoon after leaving the hospital, she even had her hair done, investing in a rinse which gave it a satin-like sheen. Extravagantly, driven by a peculiar kind of recklessness, she had, that same afternoon, invested in some new make-up and a new dress, which she couldn't really afford as she was down to the last of her savings.

If she had had any doubts about the wisdom of her overspending, they disappeared that evening when she saw the glinting appreciation in Sloan's eyes. She looked so nice that even Paula noticed immediately.

'What wonderful dress sense you have!' she exclaimed, as Stacy loosed the fur cape she had borrowed from June, 'I suppose this will be part of your cleverness with colors. You look really lovely, Stacy dear. While I lie here like a sick old woman!'

'Well, you are one,' Sloan reminded her, with what Stacy considered unnecessary bluntness.

In the plush restaurant he took her to afterwards, for all she knew sons were not always as tactful as they might be with their mothers, Stacy couldn't prevent herself from rebuking him. 'I think your mother was hurt, Sloan, when you said that to her. Was there any need to be so frank?'

'There can be a need to speak the truth, even if it does hurt, Stacy. And I was actually only confirming what she herself had already said.'

'Most women only say something like that in the hope of having it denied.'

'Usually men are not so dumb they don't know what's expected of them,' he retorted drily, 'but there comes a time when most people have to be convinced they're not so young as they used to be. One day I'll probably reach that age myself.'

'Yes, I suppose so.'

'Don't sound so reluctant to admit I might be right,' he teased. His eyes went over her, as they had been doing all evening. 'At least I do agree with Paula that you're looking beautiful.' His hand went out to cover hers as it lay on the table. 'When I first saw you, you reminded me of a dewy English rose, but tonight I see in you one of the more exotic flowers we have on the Gulf. I'm not sure which I like best. Certainly, tonight, you could very easily arouse the worst in me, and if you really are just a small, innocent rosebud, then it wouldn't do either of us much good.'

Shaken, because she wasn't sure which she wanted to be herself, Stacy tried to look away, but his eyes held hers and she felt she was drowning in their darkly audacious depth. She knew what she was and had never had any reason to regret it, but for the first time she found herself wishing she had had a little more experience. Her breath leapt in her throat, but it was Sloan who looked away first, his mouth tightening, as if he had read clearly all the information he'd been searching for. Hollowly, Stacy wished she had been ready with a smart reply, which might have encouraged his interest instead of eliminating it, as her silence had obviously done.

Yet he didn't seem so uninterested when later, after they

had danced until midnight at the club where they had dined, he pulled off the main road and kissed her. Under the screen of some overhanging branches he pulled her gently to him, his hand moving slowly over her loose, shining hair. As it slid caressingly down to her nape, her skin tingled unbearably under his firm fingers.

'Such an innocent young face,' he mocked softly, his thumb moving tenderly along her throat to her chin, turning it towards him. 'I'm almost frightened to touch you.'

Yet touch her he did, if only carefully. His head bent, his mouth brushing hers lightly. There was no pressure to open her lips. It was the faint gasp of her own indrawn breath which did this, as her heart began to race painfully.

She felt him take hold of her fur cape, pushing it aside to allow his hands free access to her back, so he could hold her closer. Then the pressure of his mouth deepened to a sudden hard, deliberate urgency, which refuted his former gentleness. The darkness about Stacy seemed split with bright flashes of light as she clung to him. His hands were moving down her body sensuously, and feeling her bones were about to break beneath the hardness of him, she moaned.

He spoke against her mouth. 'I'm trying not to hurt you.'

'I don't care.' Another day he would be gone, so why should she? In her was just a passionate desire to make the most of what must surely be a last opportunity.

He drew down the zip, a little way, at the back of her dress, so he might explore the smooth skin of her shoulders. Quickly he lifted her across his knee, so she was lying against him, his hands, no longer gentle, continuing their close exploration. Unmoving, she lay shivering against him, knowing he must feel her heart thudding as her arms clasped tighter around his neck, silently begging him to continue making love to her.

His lips were tormenting as he crushed hers hungrily. Overwhelmed by a peculiar frustration, her hand pushed at the buttons of his shirt. Obligingly he helped her, so her fingers slid easily to the bare roughness of his chest. Her lids fluttered. Dazed, as he drew back a little, she met his probing glance.

He groaned, catching her small hand to hold it tightly against his bare skin. 'I hope you know what you're doing, Stacy?'

The sudden starkness of his query, the thrusting of all responsibility, as it were, into her camp, had the same effect as a shower of cold water. Blindly she struggled away from him, her eyes wide with shame and humiliation.

'What's wrong?' he taunted grimly. 'I wasn't rejecting you. I just don't want you having second thoughts when it's too late. I can tell you want me.'

'I want to go home,' she denied. Her mouth was numb from his kisses; she only wished the rest of her felt the same way. 'I hope you understand.'

Softly he sighed, staring down at her, frowning through the semi-darkness. Then just as she feared he was going to reach for her again he turned and switched on the engine. 'Don't worrry,' he said quietly, 'it was my fault. I know what you are.'

She didn't ask him to explain that, as she was sure he could have several answers, and on all of them she could be guilty.

Back at Thorn Farm he wished her a curt goodnight and she gazed at him, her face pale with regret. 'Sloan——' she entreated, as he turned to leave her.

He halted, on his way to the office. 'We have to talk tomorrow, Stacy,' he spoke with a hint of weariness. 'Be a good girl, leave it until then. I have some calls to make, and I don't want to wake the household.'

'You—you're not too furious with me?' She knew it was a stupid question because there could be no satisfactory answer, yet somehow she had to ask it.

Surprisingly the glimmer in his eyes wasn't of anger, or

contempt, although neither could she believe it was tenderness, but his hard features did seem to soften as he came back to where she stood dejectedly at the bottom of the stairs. 'No, Stacy, I'm not furious with you; quite the opposite, in fact. I understand—and respect—and it's up to you to believe it.'

The next morning he told Stacy he wanted her to go with him to Bilton, but when they got there he confessed quite bluntly that he had only asked her there to get her away from Thorn Farm. 'Your mother uses her office and I don't want you distracted.' When Stacy looked puzzled he explained, after a moment, 'I believe you have a decision to make and I don't want you distracted because I would like an immediate answer.'

Apprehensively, Stacy walked by his side. He was leading the way to the small gate which led to the field that went with the Manor, and the change in his mood from the evening before was marked. There was a curious grimness in his face this morning, a look of brooding authority which she didn't understand, but it made her wary. It seemed obvious he was about to give an order which would be cloaked in the guise of a request, but which would not leave her much choice in the way of an answer.

At the gate she hesitated, her eyes searching his dark features, wondering why her heart should beat faster now every time she was near him. The morning air was fresh and crisp, and in his crew-necked sweater and well cut pants he looked vitally healthy and masculine. Stacy doubted, momentarily, if she would be able to deny him anything.

'Come on,' he sounded as though he had no patience with her uncertain dithering, 'we're just going to walk over the field. I'm not going to eat you—although,' he grinned, 'sometimes you tempt me.'

'Not as much as Barbara.' Oh dear, what on earth had made her say that!

Before she could apologise, he said curtly, 'So my mother's been at it again?'

'I—I'm sorry, I shouldn't have mentioned it,' she stammered uncomfortably. 'She only said there was a girl called Barbara, and she thought you—you loved her.'

His dark brows lifted suavely on her flushed cheeks, her unconsciously anxious eyes. 'If that's supposed to be a question, Stacy, you'd better forget it. I could hardly tell you before I'd told the girl, could I?'

So it was just a matter of time, and last night he had just been amusing himself. Well, it was nothing she hadn't already suspected. She tried to be philosophical as she obediently followed him through the gate and walked by his side. Dully she asked, pain wafting through her, 'What was it you wanted to speak to me about?'

'Taronda.'

'Taronda?' she queried.

'Yes.' His hand shot out as she stumbled on a piece of rough ground, and he kept a hold of her arm, as if he wanted no more untimely interruptions. He didn't accuse her, this time, of repeating things after him, but went straight on, 'You won't know yet that Paula has decided to return to Taronda for the next two or three months, until she's fully recovered and at least some of the rebuilding here has been carried out.'

'But she wasn't going back?'

'This operation has shaken her a bit,' he replied smoothly, his eyes slanting to Stacy's slightly stunned face. 'It's been a success, and physically she's in good shape, but she hasn't got quite the same resilience as a younger woman.'

'I—yes, I do see,' Stacy heard herself faltering, thinking she understood, now, why Sloan had wanted to speak to her. She was to be quietly told his mother had no further use for her, and once again the future stretched empty and desolate before her. 'Couldn't Mrs Maddison stay at Thorn Farm?' she looked up at Sloan appealingly. 'Mum would love to have her.'

'It's her own decision, Stacy,' he sounded vaguely irritated, 'I didn't push her. I don't know how a woman works these things out, but she just feels she couldn't sit around for the next few weeks in someone else's house.'

Stacy nodded, forcing herself to understand. 'I suppose you're right. Most people, Mum says, suffer some degree of depression after an operation.'

'Agreed,' he nodded briefly. 'That's why I'm happy she's coming home. I've always found it easier to recover from anything by my own fireside.'

'You don't look as though you ever have much wrong with you.' Her eyes were held by his hard, tough image, which seemed to deny that illness could ever touch him.

'No one is in the best of health or spirits all the time, my child.' His glance fastened on her clouded face. 'You don't look too happy yourself, right now. Aren't you pleased you're going to get rid of us?'

'No,' she protested, amending quickly, 'I would never think that way about your mother, but I've had a feeling,' she confessed reluctantly, 'that she would be happier convalescing at Taronda. I believe she misses it more than she'll admit. But I'll miss her ...'

'Well, you won't have to.' The hand on her arm slid to her shoulder, spinning her around abruptly. 'You're coming with her,' Sloan said, very emphatically.

'With her?'

'Yes,' slowly he considered Stacy's stunned expression, 'but she won't be able to make the journey for a little while yet, while I must leave almost at once. I've been here too long as it is. It's you who must accompany her, as she couldn't possibly make it alone. She might try, but I wouldn't give much for her chances.'

For a moment Stacy felt too bewildered to speak. It seemed inconceivable that Sloan was asking her to take his mother to Australia! It must be the chance of a lifetime, one which might never come again. At this point she took a firm hold of her feelings. He wasn't asking her to stay there. He probably only intended she should accompany his mother there, then come straight home again.

Uncertainly she asked, 'Wouldn't Mrs Maddison be better with a properly trained nurse—one experienced in travelling with invalids? I know you can get them.'

Derisively he replied, 'She won't be an invalid, Stacy, not then. You'll be able to do anything that's needed, and of course you'll stay at Taronda until she wants to come back here.'

So he did intend her to stay, and at Taronda. 'You can't really want me at Taronda?' she whispered.

'Maybe not,' he agreed enigmatically. 'But I'm not considering my own inclinations. It's much more important that Paula has someone she likes around, and especially to travel with.'

'I don't know if I could manage,' she said truthfully.

'Why not?' he asked coolly. 'It's not as if you'd never been anywhere. In spite of looking so ridiculously young, I know you're quite capable. You must have proved that in the last job you had.'

'Yes,' but this reminded her of Basil Bradley and she flinched. Yet Basil didn't seem to worry her half as much as the man standing beside her. How could she go to Taronda, knowing how she was beginning to feel about its owner? What if her feelings deepened and she found herself hurt in a different way? And she would be hurt, she was sure, when he announced his engagement to this girl Barbara. Defiantly she tried to look at him. 'I was in charge of my department, but that's not the same as having travelled.'

'I still don't think you'll finish up in Russia,' his eyes narrowed slightly but he spoke lightly. 'Anyway, Paula knows the ropes. She'll keep you right.'

'Did your mother leave the station much?' she asked.

'She was always away somewhere.'

'What about your father?'

'Stacy?' He gave her a little shake to remind her. 'You haven't actually agreed to come.'

She felt her cheeks grow pink as she realised how curious she must sound about his parents' marriage, but she doubted it, if she'd been married to a man like Sloan Maddison, if she could have borne to have left him for even a few days.

As Sloan's hands left her shoulders she disguised her thoughts, staring at him blankly. 'You ask me to go to Taronda, but you don't sound as though you're giving me much choice.'

'Not really,' a mirthless smile touched his mouth. 'I can't, of course, force you to come, but if you refuse I promise you'll regret it.'

'I could regret going even more,' she said despondently, weighed down by a prevailing certainty.

'One of the hazards of committing yourself to someone else,' he mocked dispassionately. 'You can't always consider your own feelings. You took the job, against my advice if you remember—I'm merely going to see you carry it out.'

'What makes you so sure I'll refuse?'

'You mightn't have the guts.'

'You don't believe in softening your punches, Mr Maddison!' she retorted, stung to quick anger at his insulting tones, 'but you could try a little honesty yourself. I think this is what you've had in mind all along, when you insisted I continue working for your mother after she became ill. For some reason, which we can leave nameless, you can't wait to get back to Australia, but you knew you couldn't leave your mother to manage on her own.'

Sloan Maddison showed he was just as capable as Stacy of quick anger, but his was more controlled. While his eyes blazed, his voice cut coldly. 'I don't care what the hell you think, just so long as you're convinced there's no easy way out. At Taronda you might be lonely, but I'm certainly not going to apologise for its isolation. It would be as well to remember it's a job you're on, not a pleasure jaunt, and that you can't escape from this job as easily as you apparently did from your last one.'

Her face white, as his icy fury hit her, Stacy felt quick tears spring to her eyes. 'I'm sorry,' she whispered miserably, quailing before him, knowing she had gone too far.

He eyed her grimly, then his mouth softened. 'Queensland isn't the end of the world, you know. If you think about it I'm sure you'll agree. I don't want to quarrel with you, Stacy, but you try a man's patience, you really do.'

The feeling of being neatly manipulated persisted, but she knew she must ignore it. His lovemaking last night, his anger just now, must be evidence of his willingness to go to any lengths to persuade her to look after his mother, so he could be free to leave. Hollowly she tried to concentrate on Taronda and was surprised by a quick wave of excitement. True, it was just a small wave at first, but it grew, a new friendliness on Sloan's face seeming to urge it on. 'If you give me time, I'm sure I'll begin to look forward to seeing Australia,' she said huskily.

'Perhaps I sprang it on you too quickly,' he smiled, 'but you'll soon get used to the idea, and I can promise you'll enjoy it.'

'I'm sure I shall,' she smiled back at him, raising a small, eager face to him. 'Do you think I might occasionally borrow a horse?'

He laughed, and dropped a lazy arm around her shoulders, with the ease of a man having got his own way. 'We might find you something, when I can spare the time to go with you.'

'Oh, you won't need to do that,' she protested, conscious of his arm tightening and speaking without thinking. 'I expect I'll soon be able to find my own way around.'

Sloan smiled again but didn't correct her. Instead he lowered his mouth to drop a hard kiss on her softly curved lips. When she stepped back as though burnt, he slipped the back of his hand into the front of her primrose checked shirt to pull her close again, and she felt the hardness of his knuckles against the warmth of her throbbing skin.

Blindly she struggled as his mouth pressed hers apart. Even while a fiery cyclone of desire rushed through her she was too conscious that he was only using her for his own ends. His fingers moved, but, as he turned them deftly to grasp the rounded fullness of one taut breast, she was suddenly free.

There was the sound of a car in the drive by the house, but she couldn't tell, because she was shaking too much to look at him, if that was why Sloan had let her go.

It was, and the smouldering hardness in his voice when he spoke betrayed that he could have wished the car a hundred miles away. 'It seems we have visitors?' he removed his eyes from her burning cheeks to glance past her. 'It looks like our friend the surveyor. I'd better go and see what he wants.'

'What he wants?' Stacy whispered stupidly.

'Not what you want, I'm sure,' Sloan mocked gently, but without noticeable pity for her trembling indignation as he turned away.

Later, as they returned to Thorn Farm, after he had dealt with the surveyor, he told her she must see about getting her medical shots and a passport, if she didn't already have one.

'When are you going?' she asked, suddenly apprehensive.

'Tomorrow.'

'So soon!'

'I'm overdue, as I've already told you.' He slanted her a dry glance, making her realise again that he felt no real tenderness for her. 'You sound as though you don't want me to go, but I'm sure I must be mistaken.'

'Yes,' on a wave of futile anger, Stacy spoke coldly, 'you're quite mistaken! I was simply wondering about your mother. Does she know?'

He nodded briefly. 'I told her this morning. Tonight I'll tell her you've agreed to my proposals. She'll be more than happy.'

'There doesn't seem to be anything more to say, then,' Stacy murmured stiffly.

'No, nothing,' he agreed, completely indifferent to her faint air of resentment as he swung the sleek car out onto the main road.

That evening they came straight back from Birmingham as Mrs Weldon insisted, as Sloan was leaving next day, that they all dine together. Seeing how he accepted with unusual alacrity, Stacy decided unhappily that because she had agreed to accompany his mother to Australia, the need for him to buy her expensive meals no longer existed. In the small family dining room next to the kitchen, no one seemed aware of Stacy's quietness, and if she noticed Sloan's glance sometimes resting intently on her face she simply looked the other way. Not even later, when Mrs Weldon and June went out to attend to another guest who had arrived, could she bring herself to talk naturally to him. Suddenly he seemed like a stranger again, and it dawned on her, with the sharpness of a blow, that once he was home the people whom he had met here might soon fade in significance from his memory.

Certainly Stacy's continuing silence didn't appear to bother him, and she knew he was conscious of it, even if her mother and June were not. When he left on the following morning he made no attempt to do more than shake her hand, in a distinctly businesslike manner, and murmur politely that he was looking forward to seeing her again.

Stacy went upstairs to her room, rather than wait to see him out of sight, yet somehow she was unable to resist the temptation of going to her window and watching from behind the veiled disguise of the lace curtains.

She heard her mother call a last goodbye and come back into the house as Sloan drove away. Then, just as he was leaving the yard, Richard arrived. Stacy saw the two cars stop and both men get out, Sloan walking back obviously to tell Richard he was going.

She couldn't hear what Richard said in reply, but she was surprised to see Sloan jerk stiffly upright and glance back at the house sharply. Then, after a few more brief words, he returned abruptly to his car, leaving Richard staring after him with what looked suspiciously like bewildered embarrassment.

Whatever had caused Richard's obvious discomfort Stacy, from this distance, couldn't guess. It was Sloan's expression which startled her most. As he had turned to glance up at her window, he had looked almost vicious.

That his eyes had seemed to leap in her direction might be purely incidental, but a cold uneasiness sent her flying downstairs to confront Richard. He was crossing the hall, and when she asked if he and Sloan had been quarrelling, he merely shrugged and told her she had too much imagination.

'Sloan Maddison wouldn't quarrel with the likes of me,' he said. Then, more lightly, 'He was just telling me that you're taking his mother home when she gets better, and I was just telling him how lucky she was to have you. Satisfied?'

Uncertainly, Stacy nodded, while feeling instinctively Richard was hiding something. It was unusual for him not to meet her in the eye. 'I just wondered,' she faltered.

'Well, don't,' he smiled quickly, before continuing his way to the kitchen, leaving Stacy gazing after him, knowing it would be a long time before she could forget the dark look on Sloan's face.

It seemed incredible to Stacy that just over three weeks later she should find herself on the other side of the world, in Australia. She and Mrs Maddison landed at Kingsford Smith airport, in Sydney, the capital of New South Wales.

Their last stopover had been at Singapore, where they had spent two days. Sally, Mrs Maddison's daughter, met them off the plane and drove them swiftly to where she lived, on one of the foreshores of Port Jackson.

Mrs Maddison, still not as strong as she would like to have been, decided she would stay with Sally until she felt able to complete the final stage of the journey to Taronda. Once settled, she seemed inclined to linger, and Stacy, while secretly longing to see Sloan again, felt it wasn't her place to raise any objections. Sydney was a delightful city and Sally and her husband appeared more than pleased to have them.

During the day, while her two children were at school, Sally showed Stacy around. The harbour was regarded as one of the most beautiful in the world, and to Stacy it seemed that no part of the city was very far from water. The Sydney Harbour Bridge, spanning Port Jackson, was the second largest single-span bridge to be found anywhere, and took a huge daily flow of traffic. Stacy found she liked the harbour and the beaches best, especially when they took the children. In fact, she was so good with the children, a boy and a flaxen-haired girl, that Sally told her she would be loath to part with her.

Sally was dark, reminding Stacy of her brother, so that she often found herself looking at her, eager to catch more of the faint resemblance. Although she was younger than Sloan, Sally's features were of a similar mould, and when she smiled her eyes crinkled in much the same way, but she had none of Sloan's hardness. She would never, Stacy thought, have his degree of self-sufficiency, as she seemed to rely heavily on her husband.

One afternoon Sally was telling Stacy how Bill, her husband, was planning to take them out to lunch when the phone rang. It was Sloan.

Sally had answered it. 'He demands,' she hurried back into the room, 'that you go home immediately! What's got into him, I'd like to know? He almost snapped my head off when I said you might be stopping a bit longer. He wants to speak to Stacy,' she added quickly, as her mother made to rise. 'If I were you I would stay where you are, Mother dear. Let Stacy tackle him, in the mood he's in.'

Feeling slightly embarrassed as well as apprehensive, Stacy left them. In spite of her nervousness she found a tremulous excitement gripping her, even a strange hunger, just to hear his voice again. Swallowing something in her throat, she picked up the receiver. 'Sloan?'

'Miss Weldon?'

She went a little cold at that, but of course he could be making sure. 'Speaking,' she replied, automatically, not quite so warmly this time.

He didn't ask what sort of journey they had had, but he did say sharply, 'My sister tells me my mother is much better.'

'Yes—I suppose she is, on the whole.'

'Good,' the curt tones continued. 'I'm at Cairns. I'll be here to take you home tomorrow. I'll pick you up.'

'Cairns?' she queried.

'That's what I said, Miss Weldon,' either the line or his voice crackled. 'My mother knows where it is.'

'I'm not sure if we can manage tomorrow,' Stacy protested foolishly, some of his grimness getting through to her, at last, and throwing her off balance. 'You see, your brother-in-law has arranged to take us all out to lunch.'

'Then he'll just have to cancel, won't he? Tell him I'm sorry.'

He sounded just the opposite, and knowing she was exposing herself to his anger, she retorted with spirit, 'If I remember.'

'Don't try that kind of talk with me, Miss Weldon.' To say he was cool would have been an understatement, 'Arrange your flight this afternoon and I'll see you tomorrow.'

'Very well, Sloan.'

'Goodbye, until then.'

Stacy heard the click at his end while she still held the receiver to her ear. He had rung off, cut her off in the middle of her sentence, deliberately. Tears stung her eyes, one fell and a sob escaped her as she wiped it away. Sloan had sounded so abrupt and unfriendly. There had been no 'Paula' or 'Sally'—just 'my sister', 'my mother', and that terrible 'Miss Weldon'! There had been none of the warmth he had shown her at Thorn Farm and, as she realised this, a wave of misery shook her. Hadn't she been right to suspect he had only made himself pleasant in order to persuade her to accompany his mother here? He had obviously amused himself with this in mind, and had apparently decided to make this quite clear before he met her again. It might not have mattered so much, Stacy thought bleakly, if she hadn't been such a little fool as to fall in love with him!

CHAPTER SIX

IN spite of the cold conviction that Sloan Maddison didn't want much to do with her any more, there was still a faint flicker of optimism in Stacy's heart as she and Mrs Maddison flew north next day. Whatever her private thoughts, Mrs Maddison had apparently no intention of disobeying her son, and not even Sally's somewhat heated declaration that he was getting to be unreasonable could sway her. She did, in fact, seem quite pleased to be going home, but on the big jet she talked so much about Sally that Stacy wondered if she had been more reluctant to leave her than they had realised. It made Stacy doubtful as to how she would manage when she settled in England and perhaps would see Sally no more than once a year.

Leaving Sydney, the weather had been mild, but Mrs Maddison warned that it would be much warmer at Cairns, on the north-east coast of Queensland, and even hotter as they flew west to the Gulf country. With this in her mind, Stacy had decided to wear a cool button-through cotton dress in cream, with slim, high-heeled sandals. Her hair she had pinned in a thick coil at her nape, a style which she hoped would make her look both cooler and older. She wasn't aware that it gave exactly the opposite impression, the severity of it making her slightly tilted blue eyes seem larger, her soft mouth even more vulnerable.

Arriving at Cairns, Queensland's most northerly city, Stacy felt an odd excitement leap through her as she saw Sloan coming towards them. In England he had always looked ruggedly masculine, but here, in a casual short-sleeved shirt, open almost to his waist, and a pair of thin trousers moulding his well-shaped hips, he took her breath away completely.

For a few seconds she wasn't conscious of the woman by his side. When she did notice there was someone hanging on his arm, some of the brightness faded from her face.

'Paula,' Sloan bent to place a light kiss on his mother's cheek, but apart from a brief nod made no immediate attempt to speak to Stacy.

Quickly the woman by his side stepped forward. 'Hello, Mrs Maddison. It's nice to have you back.' Before Paula could reply, like Sloan, she kissed her. Darting past Paula, this stranger's eyes dwelt on Stacy insolently.

'You haven't met Stacy.' Paula glanced sharply at her tall son, although she was clearly not speaking to him. 'Miss Weldon very kindly agreed to come with me after I'd been so ill. Stacy, this is Miss Barbara Bolam, a friend of ours.'

Stacy smiled, although her face felt stiff. Murmuring a conventional greeting, she didn't offer to shake hands as Barbara made no attempt to come near her. Out of the corner of her eye she was conscious of Sloan watching the two of them sardonically.

Barbara, a dark vision in cool navy slacks, which made Stacy feel strangely over-dressed, transferred her attention to Paula again. 'Haven't you been lucky,' she said, 'finding someone with nothing else to do? I mean, who was free to come with you. But now you're back, you won't need little Miss Weldon any more, surely? I'd be only too pleased to help all I can.'

'It's kind of you to offer, dear,' again Paula glanced at Sloan's impassive face, 'but you see, I've engaged Stacy to help with my house in England, and I don't want to lose her.'

'Ah, yes,' Barabara, smiling in the sunshine like a cat, ran her fingers up the inside of Sloan's arm, in a way which set Stacy's teeth on edge, 'Sloan did mention Miss Weldon's qualifications. If I'd been half as clever,' she purred, 'I doubt if the doing up of one small house would have satisfied me, career-wise. I'm afraid my voluntary work doesn't seem much by comparison.'

Sloan said, very appreciatively indeed, 'We've always admired everything you've done, Barbara. Never underrate yourself.'

Barbara's long lashes fluttered coyly in her perfectly made up face before she turned back to Mrs Maddison. 'I could be at Taronda next week, so you can think about it. Maybe Miss Weldon will be homesick by then. She doesn't somehow seem the right type for an Outback cattle station. Sloan doesn't think she might even stick it that long.'

'I don't give up that easily.' Anger coming to her rescue, Stacy found her tongue and stared at Sloan defiantly.

'We'll just have to see how things go.' Ignoring Stacy, he bent to kiss Barbara warmly. 'You can always look after me.'

As Mrs Maddison glanced at her dryly, Stacy made a great effort to force a carefree smile, even while everything inside her seemed to be shrivelling up. Sloan needn't think she might harbour any ideas regarding him now, but she wished him joy of Barbara! In the next half hour he saw Barbara off before getting his mother and herself on board his small private plane.

The plane, a six-seater, was fast and luxurious. 'It's no big jet,' he spoke to Stacy for almost the first time, noticing her wide-eyed admiration as she gazed around, 'but it does make a more comfortable ride for my mother than some of the smaller types.'

For his mother he had compassion and to spare. Wistfully Stacy found herself watching his broad shoulders, the proud set of his dark head, as he sat in the pilot's seat, listening to the air traffic controller. There was something in his eyes when he looked at her which puzzled her, and she thought yearningly of the occasions when he had been kind to her. She couldn't understand such a complete change of attitude, Barbara or no Barbara! As he had contrived so deviously to persuade her to come here, it was difficult to know why he felt he must go to such lengths to convince her he had no personal interest. She wouldn't have thought a man like Sloan Maddison would have bothered.

Frowning, her face paling with pain, she fumbled blindly with the seat belt he told her to fasten. She could have been mistaken. Might she not have imagined animosity where none existed? But when she lifted her head to find him glancing around at her, she felt stunned by the coldness of his expression. Her heart sank. It was exactly as she remembered it on the morning he had left Thorn Farm, and this time she knew it wasn't imagination! As his eyes went slowly over her, there was something brutally assessing in their depth which sent a shiver right through her. If he had meant to be insulting, he had succeeded, probably far better than he realised.

After this he gave all his attention to taking off, and Stacy, once she had conquered the impulse to demand to be set down so she could return to England, tried to relax. Eventually, a natural resilience taking over, she began taking a greater interest in the country over which they were flying, and a positive thrill of unexpected excitement rushed through her as she viewed the wild, desolate land below them. There were rivers flowing over wide plains, with tree-lined channels diverging from them, making grass-covered islands of dry land when these smaller streams joined the parent ones again. From the edges of some of these flood plains rose slightly higher country, and then to ridges of ancient rock, on the margins of the Eastern Highlands. Then there were more wide plains, an almost treeless landscape of rolling grasslands which stretched away to every horizon.

There seemed no end to it; plains, mountains, trees and rivers, shimmering under the harsh heat of a semi-tropical sun. Those gleaming rivers and wild plains, she had no doubt, held dangers in keeping with the roughness of the terrain, yet not even this thought could subdue a rising exhilaration. After feeling so dead inside, since the event of Basil Bradley, it was like coming alive again. The only time she had experienced anything like it was when Sloan kissed her.

Quickly she wrenched her thoughts from that. Looking down on the vast plains, she wondered why such evidence of lonely isolation should stir in her such a wonderful feeling of anticipation. It was like coming home, for all she already had one; like finding something she had been looking for all her life. What she had read about the country had given the impression of barren hostility, nothing she remembered had prepared her for the immensity, the colourful attractiveness of this wild, ancient land. It seemed to beckon her, with all the pulling power of a magnet, and, without being in any sense dramatic, she wondered if it would ever let her go.

All she had seen of Australia so far had interested her. Expecting to feel homesick, she had recovered from her first qualms very quickly. Mrs Maddison, when Stacy had confessed to feeling almost ashamed at not missing her own country more, said she had felt exactly the same way herself, and had never felt differently until her husband died. Even now, Paula had added, although she contemplated leaving it, she still loved Australia dearly.

When Paula woke from a prolonged doze an hour or two later, she said she felt ill. 'You'll have to put down somewhere, Sloan. I can't go on.' Sitting beside him, she glanced enquiringly at him. 'Where are we?'

'West of the Gregory,' he told her briefly, taking a quick look at her white face. 'I'll make for Warra Warra. Whether Ed's there or not, you'll be better there until the morning.'

'We ought to have stayed the night at Cairns,' Stacy, immediately anxious for Paula, was startled to hear herself daring to reproach him. Ed's place didn't, somehow, sound very reassuring.

'We could have done,' Sloan's voice held cold impatience, 'but we would still have had to face this journey tomorrow, with the same possibility of having to break it. It didn't make sense to waste almost an entire day in Cairns.'

Chastised, Stacy subsided, yet she couldn't help feeling a little lighter-hearted to think he hadn't grasped the opportunity of spending a few hours with Barbara Bolam. Of course Barbara might be busy with her voluntary work, and she was coming to the station next week. Some of Stacy's happier mood disappeared, as she leant forward to try and comfort Mrs Maddison.

Another half an hour and they were landing on an airstrip sliced from a piece of rough ground. Dismayed, Stacy gazed out as she released her seat-belt. There didn't appear to be any sign of a house, and none whatsoever of the man called Ed. Sloan had made a perfect landing, but she wondered if he had come to the right place.

"Haven't you made a mistake?' she asked, when he glanced around automatically to see that she was all right.

'Mistake?' he snapped.

She had a horrible feeling the mistake was hers, but she persisted, 'Well, there's nothing here.'

'If you have sense, Miss Weldon, you don't land right on top of a house. It's over there, among those trees you can see in the distance. Now give me a hand, will you, with Paula?'

He sounded so sarcastic, Stacy felt about nine inches tall as she helped to assist his mother from the plane, but rather than upset Mrs Maddison she bit back the sharp retort she had been about to make.

Sloan was speaking again. 'If you both stay here, I'll find something to take us to the homestead. There must be no one at home, otherwise they would have been here when they heard the plane.'

'Where's Warra Warra?' Stacy asked Paula anxiously as they watched him stride away from them, with the swift, lithe movement which so marked him.

'Here, dear.' Paula had been made as comfortable as possible in a patch of shade beside the plane, and her smile was a good indication that she was exhausted rather than ill. 'We're on Warra Warra now. It's the name of one of the stations Sloan owns. Ed Tyson is the man who runs it for him.'

A few more minutes and Sloan was back with a small station wagon. Once his mother was safely inside he said to Stacy, 'I'd better fetch your overnight bags from the plane. Is there anything else you want?'

'No.' She frowned at him, apprehensive for no reason she could think of. 'So we really will be staying?'

'Until morning.'

'Oh.'

'What's the matter?' He climbed into the plane, dropping the bags into her waiting arms. 'If the isolation of this frightens you, heaven help you at Taronda!'

'It's not that.'

'What is it, then?' His eyes were cold as he stared down at her, seeing how her fine satiny skin faced up flawlessly to the searching rays of a relentless sun. 'You can count on being quite comfortably accommodated—the only thing I can't guarantee is a man.'

'Why should either of these two things particularly bother me?'

'Because usually these two commodities are all a girl like you thinks about.'

'Have you taken leave of your senses!' she began, an angry, sinking feeling rushing through her.

'I do that regularly,' he jeered, 'but fortunately I always recover them in time.'

'For goodness' sake,' Paula called, 'are you two not coming?'

Tersely, as she clambered into the vehicle, Stacy said, 'You have some explaining to do, Mr Maddison.'

'No,' he returned, curtly, meeting her wide, defiant eyes, 'you're the one who's going to do that!'

She saw the derision on his face as he slammed the door, heard Paula speak to him, and Sloan answer, without taking in a word. He was too cruel, too big for one lone girl to tackle, with everything he uttered being aimed at letting her know how unimportant she was in his life. She felt slightly sick as the truth of that hit her, along with the long-suspected knowledge that she cared for him more than she had ever thought possible.

Warra Warra was a sprawling, one-storied dwelling without notable beauty. It was surrounded by the verandahs which Stacy had noticed in pictures of Outback homesteads but, apart from its size, had little to recommend it. What garden there was was almost overgrown. True, there were plenty of flowering shrubs, but these looked half wild, as if it was a long time since anyone had tended them.

Paula got down as soon as Sloan drew up, declaring she felt better, now she had her two feet on solid ground again, but would retire for the night. If Stacy would make her a cup of tea and perhaps a little toast, she would be very grateful.

While Sloan disappeared, presumably to try and check the whereabouts of the mysterious Ed Tyson, Stacy helped Paula to bed. Paula had stayed here before; she confessed to being far from enthusiastic about small planes. The best of them, and she only flew in the best, could make her feel ill and cause her to have to break her journey.

'Ed has plenty of bedrooms,' she said, as Stacy settled her comfortably. 'Actually he's used to my silly phobia and always keeps this one ready.'

'It seems a big house for one man,' said Stacy, looking around with a renewal of the vital interest which had been somewhat squashed by Sloan's frightening onslaught.

'It used to belong to a couple with a large family. Every time there was a new arrival Jed, the husband, just put another room on.'

'If there was a big family, where are they now?'

Paula sighed. 'Life on Warra Warra was never easy for

them, and when an uncle of Jed's in the south left him a good property down there, he just up and left.'

'And Sloan bought this?'

'Lock, stock and barrel. He'd always wanted it.'

'It must be nice,' Stacy said drily, as she went out, 'to always have the money to buy what you want.'

'Do you think she's going to be all right?'

Stacy was startled to find Sloan waiting outside in the passage for her. Colouring faintly, she hoped he hadn't overheard her last remark. 'I think she's tired more than anything else, but you should maybe go and see for yourself while I make some tea.'

'I'd better show you where everything is first.' His glance went over her, coming down to her feet. 'Your case is in the porch. I'd advise you to look for a pair of flat-heeled sandals, before you go through the floor boards. The ones you're wearing are sexy but not very practical.'

That might just be a casual remark, even if the hard glint in his eyes denied it. It might just sound as though he was accusing her of something, when he might have no such intention. Deciding it might be easier to give him the benefit of the doubt, she swallowed back a sharp retort, saying almost meekly, 'Yes, you could be right.'

If she was content to leave it, he wasn't. Scowling, his eyes fastened grimly on her slender, strapped ankles. 'You can forget about looking decorative when Ed's not here.'

'Ed Tyson?' she was genuinely puzzled. 'What's he got to do with it?'

'He's a man, isn't he?' Sloan taunted.

'A man?' There were shadows under her eyes as she blinked uncertainly up at him, her heart strangely cold.

'Quite a personable one, as a matter of fact, and I can't doubt your interest, seeing how you've taken the trouble to ask his name. I didn't tell you.'

Stacy shook her head, as if she couldn't take it in. 'You're joking, of course? Your mother told me this was Warra

Warra, and Ed Tyson manages it, or something.'

'He's a good manager, too, when he keeps his mind on his job. That's why I don't want him interested in the kind of girl who goes all out to wreck a man. A girl with loose morals would be no good to Ed at all.'

Unable to speak, Stacy could only stand groping for words, forced to watch helplessly as Sloan turned and strode into the kitchen. What had he meant? There could be no overlooking that he had implied some sort of personal insult. It must have been because of the way she had let him kiss her. Shamefaced, she recalled she hadn't exactly held back, and he wasn't to know she had never kissed anyone like that before. Now he wouldn't want to know, as he seemed intent on grabbing everything he could lay hands on to hold against her!

Blindly, feeling ravaged by a frightening despair, Stacy lifted her suitcase on a chair and opened it. Inside she found a pair of soft slippers and slowly took off her elegant shoes to put them on. By the time she had done this and closed the case again Sloan was back, his face coolly bland, with no indication that they had exchanged a wrong word.

'That's better.'

'I expect so.' Her reply sounded stiff, but better that than she burst into tears, and let him know he had her so strung up she couldn't think straight.

As she straightened, feeling much too small without heels to give her a boost, he drawled, 'If you're quite ready you can inspect the kitchen. You aren't very big. If I left you to explore on your own you might get lost.'

She flashed him a look which said plainly that she wished she was as big as he was, if only for the pleasure of knocking him down! For a moment she glared at him. If it wasn't very ladylike to have such primitive impulses, it did seem to relieve her feelings.

The kitchen was an odd kind of room. She tried hard to decide whether it was built on to the house or slightly detached from it, as they had to go through a kind of passage-way to reach it. Instantly, with her quick eye for colour and design, she found herself interested, and her small face lit up as she gazed around.

Sloan took this in as he told her briefly, 'There's plenty in the deep freeze.'

'Won't Mr Tyson object if we help ourselves?'

'As it's stocked with my beef he's hardly likely to.'

'I realise that,' she retorted, stung that he should think her an idiot, 'I just didn't want to run him short.'

"Oh, we allow for the occasional visitor,' Sloan smiled.

Stacy wouldn't have minded that smile if it had held any tolerance. 'Well, your mother doesn't want beef, I'm sure. She asked for something light.'

'You'd better get on with it, then.'

Trying to keep her interest on practical matters, Stacy turned her attention to the stove. She hadn't seen Sloan for over a month, which must be responsible for the deep hunger which would scarcely let her take her eyes off him. 'Have you any eggs?' she asked.

'Plenty.' He removed his glance from her seemingly ab-sorbed face and went outside. He came back with a basin full. 'I thought June was the cook?'

'I'm not too bad myself,' Stacy told him.

'Quite competent all round, I'd say.'

Again the hint that there was more to his words than was apparent. And it wasn't merely what he said; it was his eyes and the hardness of his face.

Without replying she dealt with the basic but adequate equipment, soon producing an appetising omelette, which would be sustaining without being heavy. This she arranged as attractively as she could on a tray along with a small pot of tea and some toast.

'I'll just take this in, then get you yours.'

When she returned he was drinking his second cup of tea at the square, scrubbed table. His dark head was bent, but he looked up as she came in. 'Still feeling better?'

Knowing his concern was for his mother, Stacy nodded, 'Yes, she's enjoying her tea. You must have been thirsty yourself?'

'I was.'

Picking up the large teapot, she wondered bleakly what sort of talk was this between two people who hadn't seen each other for weeks. As she asked if he would like some more, she watched him closely, so overwhelmed by a desire to be in his arms that she had to stick to the mundane in order not to betray herself.

As he shook his head she noticed he had put out some meat while she'd been gone. Pausing, she pushed back a heavy strand of hair which had escaped the neat coil at her nape. She felt hot and sticky. 'I'll begin your steak right away,' she said, 'and while it's cooking slowly, do you think I could go to my room? I'd like to change into something cooler before dinner.'

'Anything to oblige,' he shrugged, getting to his feet. 'It's easy enough to show you where you're going to sleep, but you don't have to dress up for me. I don't mind you as you are—when there's nothing better.'

'Sloan!'

But already he was through the door, forcing her to stumble after him, unable to decide how to tackle his veiled insults.

'Ed sleeps there,' Sloan indicated with his hand. 'There's a note to say he won't be back until tomorrow, by the way.'

'Isn't he frightened to stay away for the night without locking everything up?' Stacy asked.

Sloan laughed. 'I must remember to tell Ed that one!'

Colour tinted her cheeks and she felt her temper flaring. 'Well, how am I to know how you go on? I've a lot to learn.'

'Not everyone would agree with you.' Smoothly he paused at the open door of a good-sized room containing a double bed. 'Will this do? It's some way from my mother, but it's the most—er—suitable. I've slept here myself.'

'This will do fine. I don't mind where I sleep,' she assured him quickly.

'I thought you'd be harder to please,' his dark eyes burned mockingly. 'The bathroom's next door.' With which he left her.

Stacy really did break down then, if only for a minute. Tears sprang to her eyes, brimming over, her throat aching from the weight of them. Desperately she thrust her knuckles against her lips, trying to beat them back, surprised to find she was shaking. Why was Sloan acting like a horrible stranger? His hidden innuendoes, although she couldn't understand them, had not been lost on her. She felt battered by them, everything inside her hurting.

Where on earth had he said the bathroom was? Made slightly sick by her own distress, Stacy rushed unsteadily next door, her forehead damp with perspiration.

The bathroom was a gem. Her sickness receding, she leant against the door, looking at it lovingly. It was old-fashioned to a degree, but she liked it immediately. The bath and washbasin were spotlessly clean; this Ed Tyson must be an excellent housekeeper as well as a good manager. Quickly, having gained control of herself, Stacy rinsed herself down in the slightly cloudy water. Going back to the bedroom, she found a cotton skirt and cool top which she put on quickly over a fresh bra and a pair of brief panties. Sparing a careless glance at her face, she decided to do without make-up, but she brushed her hair thoroughly, until it gleamed and left it hanging about her shoulders. It wasn't so cool this way, but it would give more protection when Sloan's eyes grew too piercing.

On her way back to the kitchen she couldn't resist a quick look around. She found Sloan there. He appeared to have washed as his hair still looked damp, but this was all.

'It's a lovely house,' she said impulsively, trying wistfully to bridge the gap between them. 'I hope Taronda is like this.'

Sloan's thick brows lifted, but he made no comment.

Swallowing, Stacy tried again. 'Your mother is asleep. I've just looked in.'

'Yes. She took two sleeping tablets and went out like a light. I doubt if she'll stir before morning. I brought out her tray—you'll notice she's eaten everything.'

Trying to infuse a little warmth in her voice, Stacy said, 'I think she's really glad to be home.'

'I'm going to see she stays.'

Stacy looked up, frowning. 'You're very protective,' she said uncertainly.

'There's a lot she has to be protected from,' he declared enigmatically.

The steak had thawed rapidly, but it took a while to cook. While it did, Stacy prepared some soup from a packet, perking it up a little with some tips she had picked up from June. All the time she was conscious of his eyes following her, dark, speculative eyes which unaccountably made her uneasy.

Eventually he went to find some cans of beer, and she was so thirsty she accepted when he passed her one. 'How big is Warra Warra?' she enquired, as the silence grew tense.

'A few hundred thousand acres.'

'Gosh, that sounds big!' she exclaimed, childishly astonished.

'It is.'

She noticed, as he took a swill of beer, the movement in his strong brown throat. 'It's not exactly a smallholding.'

'No,' he rubbed the back of his hand across his mouth, 'but it only supports about five head of stock to the square mile and, in a bad drought, it can be a loser. Taronda isn't usually such a challenge, and we can carry around sixteen head or more to the square mile. But then it's in a different area.'

'I see,' said Stacy, feeling totally ignorant. 'It's rather different from England. Not even our largest estates would have as many acres as you have here on one station.'

'Well, no, but you're talking of another kind of farming altogether. In the south, of course, we have farms more comparable with the sizes in the U.K., but from here to the west coast, right through the Northern Territory, through Western Australia you have the big sheep and cattle stations, sometimes over a million acres. Hot, dry land, most of it, and in Western Australia, where you have the deserts—the Gibson, the Great Sandy, the Simpson, to name just three—sometimes it doesn't rain in years. We don't usually have such droughts here, in the Gulf country, but we can have serious flooding. My father used to tell me how, a few years before I was born, a storm swept twenty thousand cattle out to sea.'

'His?' Stacy felt horrified at such numbers.

'Fortunately not.'

A little sigh of relief went through her, to be replaced by something near frustration. 'I suppose Miss Bolam doesn't need to be told any of this. She must know everything there is to know about your cattle stations?'

'Her father owns one.'

'So it follows,' Stacy muttered hollowly, almost to herself, 'that she'll marry into one.'

'It will be a fortunate man who persuades her,' Sloan smiled.

'Yes.' Stacy could have overlooked anything but that smile! Hastily she jumped to her feet to cook the pancakes she had whipped up before they'd started to eat. In the larder she found some syrup which she warmed to pour over them.

'Quite delicious,' Sloan's eyes taunted her. 'Imagine, if we hadn't stopped off here, I might never have known!'

'Proof that every cloud has a silver lining.' Stifling her incredible hurt, Stacy tried to sound flippant.

'Not every one of them.'

The black mood was back, lying on him like a shadow she couldn't penetrate. Still she tried. 'I'd like to think so.'

'The incurable optimist.' Sourly he considered her. 'I think it's a bit late in the day for that.'

'Sorry, I'm not with you.'

'Because you aren't very bright,' his eyes sparkled angrily, 'otherwise you wouldn't get in half the scrapes you do.'

Bewildered a little, Stacy tried to sort that one out. 'At least I couldn't be held responsible for the one I'm in now!'

'No.' Abruptly he stood up. 'How about turning in? I'd like to make an early start, if Paula's all right in the morning.'

'Go on, then. I'll just do the dishes.'

'Leave them.'

'Oh, I couldn't!' Her eyes went over the dirty plates and pans in dismay. 'Whatever would Mr Tyson think if he was to come home unexpectedly?'

'I'm not over concerned, Stacy. Just leave them. Do as you're told.'

'You aren't my boss,' stubbornly she began piling dishes in the sink.

'You're making a mistake there.' He allowed her to run cold water over them. 'While you're here you do as I say. My mother would never dispute it. I happen to be boss at Taronda and you'd be wise to remember.' His hand came out to turn off the tap. 'Now off to bed, and that's an order.'

'Yes, Mr Maddison.' She regretted the soft sarcasm in her voice as she dried her wet hands on a rough towel, for she still had no real wish to quarrel with him. 'If there's nothing else you want, I'll say goodnight.'

He didn't answer, and she didn't look at him again as she edged past him. As he was big and this part of the kitchen small, it wasn't an easy feat to accomplish without touching him, something which her tense nerves wouldn't allow her to do.

Peeping in on Mrs Maddison, Stacy found her fast asleep, so continued to her own room. She felt tired and not a little depressed. Tomorrow, she hoped, would find her refreshed and more able to cope with everything.

Washing was difficult under the old-fashioned shower, but she was grateful for the reviving coldness of the water. Drying herself quickly, she slipped into her thin robe before picking up her clothes, so as to leave the place tidy. As Mrs Maddison was on the other side of the house, Stacy concluded that Sloan would be sleeping somewhere near her. All the same, she wouldn't risk him coming in here and falling over bits of feminine underwear.

Back in her room, she was about to take off her robe to put on her nightdress when the door opened. It was Sloan.

'Oh,' she blinked, 'I didn't hear you knock.' She tightened her sash again, her blue eyes widening. 'Is it your mother?'

'She's flat out. She won't stir until sunup.'

'Then,' Stacy felt a peculiar heat under her skin as, tall and dark, he towered above her, 'why are you here?'

'You're a cool one,' his dark brows lifted. He surveyed her ironically. 'I should have thought you would have welcomed me with open arms. Can't I expect the same privileges as Basil Bradley?'

'Basil Bradley!' Stacy repeated, like one in shock, her face white. So this was the reason for Sloan's icy disapproval. How easily, after all, it was explained! Somehow Sloan had found out about Basil Bradley, and it wasn't hard to see what conclusions he'd jumped to. He'd been expressing his contempt ever since she had got off the plane in Cairns.

'Who told you about him?' she whispered, trying to stop her hands trembling, her eyes wide with fright.

'I'm afraid your future brother-in-law did,' Sloan said curtly. 'I'd just finished telling him briefly that you were bringing Paula home, and he said, "Oh, good. Just what Stacy needs to help her get over that affair with Basil Bradley".'

'Richard said that!'

'Words to that effect.' Anger hardened the eyes fixed cynically on her face. 'He didn't speak intentionally, I'm sure, but I was just leaving and I believe the whole thing took him by surprise. In fact I think he would have given anything to have taken it back. The poor man looked most embarrassed, but this is the way this sort of thing often happens.'

CHAPTER SEVEN

'WHAT did he say exactly?' Weakly, Stacy tried to lift her chin, not wanting to give the impression that she was almost overcome with guilt, but one look at the contempt on Sloan's face made her wish she hadn't.

'That was all.'

'So you don't know any more?' She licked her dry lips. 'If you have time to listen, I'll tell you the whole story.'

'I'm afraid I know it already,' he said flatly, 'so it's no use casting around in that ingenious little mind of yours for a likely excuse. I took the trouble to investigate before I left England. If it hadn't been for my mother I might not have bothered, but where she's concerned I don't take risks.'

'What did you do?'

Sloan's smile was very unpleasant. 'It's no use whispering,' he jeered. 'You should feel relieved you don't have to pretend any more. I went straight to Birmingham.'

'But you were leaving the country that day!'

He shook his head. 'I had some business in London which I decided to forget. Instead I went to Birmingham and found the store where I remembered you'd said you had worked.'

Stacy hung her head, humiliation washing over her. 'I could have saved you the bother, if you'd come to me. I would have told you about it any time, if I'd thought you'd be interested.'

'If I'd be interested!' Black rage smouldered in his eyes. 'My God, what did you think I would be! I imagined you an innocent young woman, then to find this out!'

Stacy was cold with apprehension. 'What did you find out?'

'A lot I'd rather not repeat. A woman in your old department put me in the picture, after I'd bought her several drinks. Someone called Palmer.'

'She was always jealous because I got the job she was after.'

Indifferently he shrugged. 'Maybe, but you can't blame her for what happened, and I've reason to be grateful. She told me the lot.'

'I bet she did!'

Like chips of ice, his eyes surveyed the feverish colour in Stacy's cheeks. 'She told me how you'd teased Basil Bradley until he was nearly out of his mind. That no one was too surprised to see you running, half naked, from his office, after his fiancée found you in his arms.'

'You believed all this?'

'The facts, Stacy, tied up too well for me not to. You were thrown out and hid behind the pretence of illness, not the other way around, which was more or less what I was led to believe.'

'But it wasn't like that!' she pleaded hoarsely.

He laughed harshly. 'I'm not such a fool as to swallow everything I hear, but can you deny you came running from Bradley's office?'

'No. . .'

Grimly he cut in, 'You see, you can't deny it.'

Desperately, Stacy interrupted, 'That bit might be true, but the rest of the story wasn't. He asked to see me. How was I to know he was about to attack me?''

'You must have guessed he was near breaking point?'

'You're crude!' Her breathing was ragged, as he forced her to recall things she had tried to forget. 'He had been paying me some attention, I admit, but I'd never given him any encouragement.'

'Wouldn't it encourage him, just knowing your reputation? How you were willing to sleep around in order to advance your career.'

'I've never!'

'No?' His hands went out to take hold of her, his voice silky with insinuation. 'There's only one way you might hope to prove the truth of that.'

'No!' She jerked back from him before he could touch her. The way he was staring at her made her frightened. Shivering, she retreated even further, until she came up against the wardrobe. 'You can't be serious?' she gasped, realising suddenly that words were the only defence left to her. 'Think of your mother!'

He came towards her, so close she couldn't move, until she was wholly hypnotised by the blackness of his eyes. 'I'm thinking of her all the time,' he said angrily. 'How do you think I feel, knowing I've let her employ a girl like you?'

So that was it? It was his mother. Of course the kind of society people like the Maddisons moved in would preclude any open scandal. Sloan might indulge in discreet affairs on the side, but he would see to it that no hint of these reached his mother. To employ a girl almost publicly accused of having loose morals like herself would never be considered.

'You don't have to worry,' she choked, knowing how futile it was to protest any more, and feeling suffocated by the nearness of him. 'I can go straight back home. You can easily make some excuse to your mother. The wonder is,' she exclaimed bitterly, 'that you allowed me to get this far in the first place!'

'There wasn't time to get anyone else,' he said curtly, 'or I should have done. I had to get back here and she was still in hospital, relying on you. The whole situation was laced with pitfalls, too complicated to be sorted out in minutes, but if I hadn't implicitly trusted your mother and June things might have been different.'

That hurt, while the savagery in his eyes sent her into near panic. 'Your mother's home now, so I can leave. You

don't have to stay here. You couldn't make it plainer what
you think of me.'

'You'll certainly leave,' he agreed, 'but not immediately.
She still needs time. In a week or two, when she's properly
settled, I'll think of some excuse to get rid of you.'

'I won't wait that long.'

'Yes, you will,' his eyes were on her trembling lips, 'but
don't worry, I'm not sentencing you for life. I won't wait
until she's strong enough to rush back to Bilton Manor
with you. But let me warn you, Stacy Weldon, while you're
on Taronda, if I ever catch you so much as looking at a
man, you'll live to regret the day you were born!'

He was so deliberately insulting she shrank. 'Please,
Sloan, you must listen!' Her voice was unsteady, but she
had to do something to ease the terrible tension between
them. 'You've got to believe . . .'

'Stacy,' he jeered, his hands on her shoulders straying
to her head, holding her firmly in his long, lean fingers,
'looking at you, those wide blue eyes of yours, your soft,
enchantingly innocent mouth, on one would believe you
capable of leading a rotten life. How many men would
have to make love to you before it showed?'

As she stood, numb with frozen despair, his right hand
slid down her nape, to lightly ease the soft robe away from
her neck, his thumb finding the vulnerable hollow at the
base of her throat, rubbing gently the warm skin, coming
to rest on the throbbing vein. His movements were controlled but so powerfully erotic that she watched him
breathless, unable to move.

The dark eyes moved upwards to fix on her quivering
mouth and she was frightened of all the emotions which
threatened to take charge of her. 'So beautiful,' he murmured, 'to be so corrupt. Yet it makes you that much more
exciting.'

She shuddered, knowing he wanted to hurt her. 'Let me
go,' she begged, 'you can't really mean what you're saying!'

Sloan's voice thickened. 'Is that the formal plea which usually eases your conscience regarding the misuse of your body? Why should I let you go? I've wondered how you would look without clothes. I realise you must sometimes have been issuing a free invitation, so why shouldn't I take advantage of that offer now?'

His hand left her throat to part the front of her robe and, panic-stricken, she began fighting at last to get away from him, but her struggles seemed only to incense him. As if on the strength of her loose reputation, he found her reactions insulting, he pushed her back against the jutting wood of the wardrobe. Without mercy he held her there, a prisoner against hard chest and muscular, probing thighs. When she tried frantically to escape him he merely bowed his head to catch her shaking mouth under his, crushing her lips so barbarically that she cringed, nearly fainting.

His lips eased her mouth open as his hands strayed to where her sash had loosened, seeking the warmth of her firmly rounded body. If she had hoped to escape him it was too late. She was imprisoned as much by the rising tide of her own sensual nature as by anything else. Her heart raced heavily as she felt his increasing urgency, and her own arms began helplessly to cling to him, her hands seeking to explore as intimately as his.

A peculiar excitement went through her as she felt the vibrations attacking the limbs pressed against her. His mouth moved damply over her cheek to her shoulder before pursuing its erotic journey to her heaving breast. For an instant, as his mouth groped, he hurt her, then everything inside her tightened, took fire. 'Sloan,' she whispered, knowing he must be aware of her trembling. Knowing she should resist him yet not able to, tears of helplessness squeezed through her tightly closed lashes to fall on his cheek.

'My God!' Her voice and tears jerked him upright, his

lithe movement comprised entirely of self-disgust. There was no pity in him for the drooping girl in his arms as he thrust her from him and swiftly left the bedroom.

Believing Sloan Maddison to be a man of some sensibility, Stacy hadn't expected him to refer to her supposed indiscretions again. At least not straight away, not over breakfast next morning when she felt almost ill.

She had risen early to cook breakfast. Mrs Maddison had stayed in her room while Stacy and Sloan shared a silent meal at the kitchen table. Apart from a cold good morning he hadn't spoken to her.

Now he said, 'I'll see you get back to England as soon as possible, Stacy. The sooner you're out of my life the better.'

'Yes,' she didn't pretend not to understand, but looked down at her cup, wondering miserably why he thought it necessary to repeat himself. Surely he had made it quite clear last night! He must be making doubly sure she understood.

A slight commotion outside heralded the approach of Mrs Maddison. Like them she was ready to leave. Her eyes went quickly from Sloan to Stacy's strained face. 'Are you all right, dear?' she asked sharply.

'Yes, of course,' Stacy managed a smile though her heart felt like lead.

Sloan got to his feet. 'Come on, let's get out of here,' was all he said.

Later in the day, when they arrived at Taronda, Stacy received a distinct shock. Because she hadn't slept the night before, she was tired and dozed on and off, the bad dreams which haunted her as she did so, causing her to waken with a distressed cry. As he heard the whimper which escaped her, Sloan's head had turned quickly, but he had made no comment.

West of the blue grass, brown-topped plains of the Flinders they reached the lusher stretches of the Leichhardt River. Mrs Maddison pointed it out to Stacy as some of the best of the Gulf Country. And the worst, she had added with a resigned shrug, as though she knew all about the hopes and the heartache which went into it.

Then they arrived at Taronda. To Stacy it looked beautiful, completely different from the barren escarpment of Warra Warra. It was set like a jewel among gardens and trees, the house itself being much larger than the one they had left that morning. She felt embarrassed that she had imagined the two places would be similar. Taronda looked more like an English country house and was surrounded, at a little distance, by what appeared to be a veritable village of smaller houses and sheds and yards. Catching a glimpse of Sloan's eyes as they flew over it, she sensed his pride in his heritage, and wondered, as she was to do again and again, how his mother could even bear to think of leaving it.

Inside the house she met the housekeeper, who came immediately to welcome them. Stacy found herself moving in a kind of daze, scarcely conscious of what she said or did. There were wide rooms, she saw, all comfortably furnished, many of the paintings and decorations being impressive. There was certainly no lack of money here, nor any notable stinting over the spending of it.

The housekeeper, Mrs Turner, after a few quiet words from Sloan, conducted Stacy up the wide, shallow staircase which led from the hall. When she was shown her room she almost gasped, it was so pleasant. At least Sloan wasn't extracting revenge this way. Her expert eye recognised the quality of the creamy carpet, the satin bedcovers, the flowered chintzes which hung at the windows over an abundance of nets, designed to keep out the worst of the heat when temperatures soared.

Mrs Turner, a woman with an impassive but friendly face, said Mrs Maddison had her own suite of rooms on the ground floor, but that Sloan was next door. 'I hope you'll be comfortable,' she smiled, as she went out.

Stacy's first impulse to find Sloan and ask for a room in another part of the house died. It wasn't the sort of thing, she discovered, she could ask him now. He might only laugh, and why should she risk his cold amusement? Judging from its appearance, the room must usually be used as a guestroom. Other people besides herself must often sleep here. Sloan was hardly likely to pursue her with amorous intentions, not after his rejection of her last night, and now he had seen her, a plain little working girl, against his autocratic background, he would soon put her completely out of his mind. Unconsciously Stacy sighed, as she washed and changed before going downstairs again to find Paula.

For the next few days she saw little of Sloan. When they met at mealtimes, apart from a few conventional words, he ignored her, and she could think of nothing to say to him. It was as if a kind of barrier had been erected between them which nothing could penetrate. If Stacy found him looking at her, his eyes were hooded and blank. Only once did she suspect anger in the dark glance which he trained on her.

Paula noticed, but didn't apply any unusual significance. 'It's just because of Bilton Manor,' she said, 'He's sure to come round if we give him time, never fear.'

If Stacy wasn't sure about this, it could have been because she wasn't sure of anything any more. Mrs Maddison sometimes spent all day working on plans for her new home, continuing throughout dinner. Stacy could see this annoyed Sloan by the way his mouth tightened. She could have told him his mother didn't talk about Bilton all the time. There were many days when she refused to mention it and brooded in her rooms like a woman with a problem.

Stacy was surprised one morning, on one of these days when Mrs Maddison didn't want her, to see Sloan approaching as she wandered down by the creek. She had felt free to wander as she thought he was out with some of his men branding cattle, which removed the fear of running into him. Loving him as she did, the less she saw of him the better!

Quickly she averted her eyes, hoping he would ride straight past, but he stopped beside her. 'I want a word with you about my mother.' He stared down on her from the back of the powerful stallion he was riding, a frown marring the hard handsome lines of his face.

Self-consciously, Stacy moved beneath his intent regard. She was wearing yellow cotton jeans with a soft creamy top, and looked slim and shapely. Taronda suited her. She had been doubtful about the heat of this semi-tropical part of Queensland at first, but soon found she loved it. It seemed to bring her alive, so that her energy and natural vitality increased and she blossomed. If it hadn't been for the dark shadows of unhappiness under her eyes, the strain in a too tightly held mouth, she would have looked like any lovely, uncomplicated young girl.

Her hand went out to the horse. Unable to come to terms with the urgent desire Sloan aroused, she tore her eyes from him, and concentrated on the horse. Sloan had promised she could ride at Taronda but he had never mentioned it since she arrived. Now, as she held out her hand with undisguised longing, he snapped, 'Be careful, he isn't a pet.'

'What's his name?' she asked, with soft stubbornness, trying to ignore Sloan's sharpness.

'Grady. It means noble. My mother named him,' he said stiffly, sliding to the ground.

Again Stacy tried not to look at Sloan too closely. He was different here from what he had been in England. It might be the more casual clothes he wore which gave him such an aura of strength and power, but whatever it was it made her shiver. Sometimes it made her quake even more to think she had ever dared defy him.

'What did you want to speak to me about?' she asked meekly, studying the ground.

He didn't beat about the bush. 'You don't appear to be making much attempt to change my mother's mind about going back to England. She seems just as keen as ever.'

'I didn't realise you actually wanted me to persuade her against it.'

'You know very well that's why I allowed you to stay, but instead of getting on with it, I find you wandering idly by the creek.'

Nervously, Stacy curled her tongue over dry lips. 'She didn't want me this morning. She said she was tired and would stay in bed. Actually,' she confessed impulsively, 'I don't think she really does want to live at Bilton so much now. It's just a feeling I have, but I'm almost sure of it.'

'How sure?'

'Oh, well, we couldn't know for certain until she actually says so, but if I left I feel quite sure she wouldn't try to come with me.'

'You feel, you think,' Sloan's voice was softly sarcastic. 'I'm afraid that's not good enough, Stacy. I've warned you before that you won't leave Taronda until I'm convinced my mother won't follow you, and I'm warning you again.'

'I—I understand.' Sloan's boots were beautifully fashioned out of leather. Trying to stop herself suffering, Stacy studied them.

Without warning his fingers caught the underside of her chin, jerking it up. His eyes glinted as, startled from her prevailing caution, she met them. 'I won't talk to the top of anyone's head, Stacy. At Warra Warra we reached an understanding. Don't think you can ignore it by pretending I'm not here.'

'I don't, believe me!'

'Such an impassioned little speech,' he taunted, 'and it could mean anything. I can't even trust what I read in your eyes any more.'

Then he mightn't believe she felt mortally wounded! Urgently she tried to twist her chin from his grasp, rather than betray a longing to turn her mouth against his hand. 'Was there anything else?' she asked hoarsely.

'Ah, yes.' Unexpectedly he let go of her, pulling himself back a step. 'We're invited to a party. Paula doesn't know yet as it just came over the set. I'm not keen to turn you loose on our friends, but people will think it strange if you don't appear.'

'What kind of party?' Paula had promised there would be plenty, but this was the first Stacy had heard of.

'A twenty-first.'

Attempting futilely to revenge the hurt she had received, she said with a flicker of her old spirit, 'I wouldn't have thought this would be in your league.'

'I can assure you, the young lady in question doesn't look on me as an uncle.'

Stacy flushed and dropped her head. The young lady couldn't be much younger than herself. It had been a foolish remark to make. She understood Sloan would be one of the matrimonial catches of the State, but without his financial status she guessed he would still be popular with women. His sensual magnetism could not be mistaken, and she had seen for herself the attention he had attracted every time she had been out with him.

Sloan grabbed her arm, shaking her upright again, as if he disliked her drooping all over the place. In his eyes was cold anger. 'If you think I'm too old, how about your friend Basil Bradley?'

'I've told you,' she whispered, as his fingers tightened unmercifully, 'he wasn't my friend.'

'My God!' he taunted, 'you do make me sick. I thought women at least made friends first with the men they went to bed with!' His eyes rested on the gentle tilt of her breasts and his voice thickened. 'I supposed you need nothing more than your delightful little body to persuade them?'

Swaying as if he had struck her, she cried, 'You really believe I chased after Basil, don't you?'

'Facts, my dear, Stacy, usually speak for themselves. If no one in the store believed you, the evidence must have been indisputable.'

She half sobbed, staring at him wildly, 'Don't you see!

It was just my word against Basil's, and he's assistant managing director!'

He looked at her grimly. 'I didn't come here to be persuaded of anything. I'm just grateful I learnt what you are, so leave it. If I'd any sense I'd have you out of here before you could do any more damage. As it is, I'll have your promise, for what it's worth, that you'll behave yourself at the party. Not for my sake, for Paula's.'

Stacy nodded her head, too sick to argue with him, especially when she knew she wasn't going. What would be the use with his contempt lying on her like a brand all evening?

'I'm glad you see sense.' His voice was so harsh it seemed to grate on the silence around them. Tears dampened Stacy's long lashes. 'Remorse, or tears of hate?' Sloan laughed cynically, drawing a careless finger over them.

Glancing up at him, she shivered, only seeing him through a blur of tears which missed the derision in his eyes. 'Sloan?' She also missed the entreaty in her voice, the yearning on her face as she swayed towards him. When he bent his head and kissed her hard, her lips parted in a sigh and she put her hands to the back of his neck, slipping her fingers urgently through his dark hair.

He pushed her away, causing her to half fall against the bank where they had been standing. Mounting Grady, he swung the horse around to stare down at her, as he had done when he had first arrived a few minutes ago. Then, without a backward glance, he rode off.

Paula announced after lunch that she was off to rest, to get herself fit for the coming party. These parties, she told Stacy, were usually hectic and they always went on until the next day. Stacy asked if she thought it wise to go, so soon after her operation, but Paula merely laughed and said she wouldn't miss it for anything. She didn't look quite so happy when she remembered that Sloan had said Barbara

Bolam might be coming back with them, but this certainly didn't appear to deter her.

On her way to her room Stacy was startled to find Sloan coming out of his. She glanced at him, her pulse leaping as she recalled the way he had kissed her. Surely he couldn't hate her that much? If only she had some means of convincing him that Basil Bradley had never touched her; if only she had some evidence! If she were to offer herself to him, could she prove it that way?

As he paused beside her this was enough to bring a wave of scarlet to her pale cheeks. She looked down in shaking fear that he might read her thoughts. 'Are you going for a rest, too?' he asked suavely, as though he had never seen her since breakfast, and they had never exchanged a wrong word.

'I might,' said Stacy, having no such intention, but too confused to think of anything else.

'Would you like me to join you?' he mocked, his eyes on the open neckline of the cool dress she had put on for lunch.

'No,' but she put a hand over her heart to hide its pounding, for hadn't her thoughts been wandering on just such lines?

'No need to get in such a state about it,' he mocked, 'I wasn't serious. I happen to be particular whom I sleep with, and this afternoon I have work to do.'

Waves of misery threatened to choke her, but she swallowed them back. 'You were going to take me riding?'

'I've changed my mind,' he said curtly.

Disappointment joined the other bleak emotions which overwhelmed her. Wistfully she raised her eyes. 'I love horses, Sloan, I really do.'

'I said no, Stacy.'

'Any old thing would do,' she entreated, ignoring the angry look in his eyes.

'We don't have anything like that.' Impatient with her

insistence, his eyes sparked. 'Learn to be content with what you have, Stacy. Go and find something else to amuse yourself with.'

That evening, before dressing for dinner, Stacy lay in the bath a long time, just thinking. During the afternoon she had gone for another walk, collecting some wild flowers to press, which she hadn't been able to resist. After this she had wandered until she was tired, all the time wishing she had a horse so she might have explored further afield. When at last she had returned to the house Mrs Turner had declined her help and Mrs Maddison would talk only of the forthcoming party.

She thought she had got over Basil Bradley, but discovered she felt worse than ever. Her friendship with Sloan Maddison had never stood a chance. He would never believe her side of the story, and without trust nothing was possible. He even considered her a threat to his mother, a definite source of danger to Taronda's long-standing respectability, and there was no way she could convince him otherwise. Falling in love with him had been bittersweet, but nothing could ever come of it. As she got out of her bath and slowly dried herself she sighed deeply. If Sloan thought she wasn't fit to be near decent people, she couldn't altogether blame him, for the evidence weighed heavily against her.

When dinner was almost over Mrs Maddison asked, 'Did you go riding after lunch, Stacy? I forgot all about it.'

'No.' Without looking at Sloan, who she sensed was staring at her, she explained briefly, 'I changed my mind.'

Sloan, immaculate and disturbing in a pale shirt and dark tie, drawled sardonically, 'It doesn't seem worthwhile for the short time Stacy will be here.'

'Well, for goodness' sake,' Paula exclaimed impatiently, 'if we were just here for three days there'd still be time to go out at least once.'

'She could be after something more exciting.'

Stacy's head jerked in his direction, to meet head-on the coldness of his eyes, the mocking smile on his lips. Her own froze. 'You know that's not true!'

'Probably. But I'm in no way convinced.'

Because she didn't want to quarrel in front of his mother, Stacy excused herself as soon as possible and went to the garden. She felt she must have some fresh air. Quickly she walked down the path between the tall flowering shrubs, skirting the swimming pool, which she hadn't yet tried, continuing on until she came to the boundary fence. Leaning against it, she breathed deeply. Here there seemed nothing between her and eternity but vast open spaces and pure cool air. It was April, one of the nicest times of the year in this part of Australia, with the days pleasantly warm and the nights comfortable. The dry, everyone called it, but warned that it would get much warmer, with temperatures reaching a hundred for weeks on end as they got nearer October. Well, she wouldn't be here in October, so why worry?

Footsteps came over the grass behind her and she thought she recognised Sloan's firm tread. She tensed, standing quite still, hoping, whoever it was, they would go straight past.

They didn't. It was Sloan and he stopped beside her. 'I wondered where you'd got to,' he said coolly. 'You have a habit of disappearing.'

Her pulse raced, as it always did now when Sloan approached her. It wasn't a comfortable sensation, this feeling that her senses were about to take over, and she fought against it. 'I was enjoying the solitude,' she replied pointedly.

He was too hardened to take hints. As he leaned with her over the railings, his strong profile was etched against the semi-darkness as he lifted his head to follow the direction of her eyes. 'You like Taronda, Stacy?'

'You know I do.' There was no attempt at prevarication; the cry came from her heart.

'Was it a case of love at first sight?'

'Yes.' Again she had to be entirely honest, but his next question startled her.

'Then why the mixture of starry-eyed misery?'

'I—I'm afraid I don't follow. What are you getting at?'

He swung on her harshly. 'I suppose you're missing Bradley like hell, and loving Taronda more than you dreamt possible. Which must account for the impression you give of being torn in two.'

Closing her eyes for a moment, she prayed for strength. 'I must go back, your mother might need me.'

The dark eyes were fixed on her face, the glitter in their depth hard as diamonds. 'You've developed quite a conscience where she's concerned, haven't you? If it hadn't been for what I know about you I might have said you would have made her a good daughter.'

The peculiar inflection in his voice evaded Stacy. She heard only the condemnation. 'You can't forget that, can you?'

'I might be tempted to,' he drawled grimly, 'but I've learnt never to ignore the rotten apple. Instead of improving it only contaminates, if it's not immediately thrown out.'

'Just as long as you're sure you aren't making a mistake,' she said hollowly.

'Mistake?' His cynical laughter rasped, then he paused, his voice icy. 'Were you in love with Bradley, Stacy? Was that it?'

As she looked at him fearfully, all her old horror of Basil Bradley returned. How could even Sloan Maddison, with all his uncaring ruthlessness, talk of love and Basil Bradley in the same breath? Sickness welled up inside her, fighting to become a physical reality. Weakly she fought it, pressing a hand hard against her throat. 'I'd rather not talk about it.'

Cruelly he jerked her around, no patience in him for her muffled protest. 'Yesterday you accused me of not listening. Well, here I am, all ready and waiting for the true confession.'

'A lot of good it would do me,' she whispered bitterly.

'We all know the one about getting it off your chest.' Insolently his eyes went to that part of her anatomy, noting her agitation.

'Why should I satisfy your curiosity?' Stacy could feel in him the desire to hurt. Sloan sensed his power over her. If he wasn't quite sure yet of its source, he knew he had the whip hand. He must never know how the love she felt for him added so surely to the torture, every time he taunted her.

'For God's sake,' he jeered, 'can't I know how it all began? I have the first line. You didn't love him, but you led him on. It's not fair to stop there.'

White to the lips, Stacy bent her head so he shouldn't see, but as usual he had no compunction about jerking her chin up. 'I didn't!' she protested, on a sob.

Suddenly his voice dropped and his hands swept the long hair back from her face, so he could see it more clearly. 'I might be willing to pay more than your managing director, to get you from under my skin. After you leave here.'

Their eyes met and there was anguish in hers. 'Never!'

The mocking smile was back on his lips. 'Don't turn me down straight away,' he advised. 'I could be worth thinking about. There are places I know where we could disappear and no one would be any the wiser.'

'I've told you, no!'

'What a cute little actress, even down to the tears! Can you wonder that I'm curious to find out for myself what makes you tick? That girl in the shop didn't doubt that men liked you.'

'Just let me go, please!'

He did, quite suddenly, and she moved to the shadow of the tree behind her, until her legs grew strong enough again to cross the lawns to the house. She had hoped Sloan wouldn't follow, but he did, and her heart continued beating with a terrible despair. If he went on insulting her she might break down completely.

He moved in close, his hands sliding over her shoulders, as if he considered her loose morals gave any man the right. When she tried to escape she found herself up against the tree trunk, unable to move.

'What do the Basil Bradleys of this world have that I don't?' he mused. 'You say you don't like me, but I haven't always received this impression. I suppose, like all women, you like to think it's the man who's doing the chasing. Next you'll be accusing me of giving you every encouragement.'

'If you did, I know why,' she exclaimed. 'It was simply that you wanted my help to try and stop your mother from settling in England. Then, after she was ill, you had to persuade me to bring her to Taronda. Considering everything, if you now believe you wasted a lot of time and charm, you have only yourself to blame.'

'Don't remind me,' he retorted curtly.

'But you remind me all the time!' she whispered bleakly. 'This is a wonderful country, but you won't let me enjoy it. I didn't expect to be here long, but now I would leave tomorrow if I could.'

'Dear me!' he mocked, 'such passion! Just when I thought I was showing the right kind of interest.'

'You'd never do that!' she replied, with a kind of desolate weariness.

'How right,' he jeered, and dropping one of his hard kisses suddenly on her mouth, increasing the pressure so that her head was spinning when he released her. 'Maybe,' he said coldly, his hand steadying her, 'you'll be more willing to co-operate next time I ask about Basil Bradley. As for leaving here, it's not very convenient right now. I'm afraid I'm much too busy to take you.'

CHAPTER EIGHT

WHEN Stacy came down to lunch next day she had on a pale blue dress in a soft, cool cotton, and on her slender arched feet she wore high-heeled white sandals. She had intended leaving her hair loose, but decided it might be cooler in a thick plait over her smooth, bare shoulders. So she did it this way, little dreaming how young and exotic it made her look with her dramatic colouring. The paleness of her dress emphasised the deeper blue of her eyes, and her slight tan the beauty of her unblemished skin.

Sloan was there for lunch. Stacy gathered, from what he was saying to his mother, he had been in the office all morning with his manager, but was going out after he had eaten. Stacy found herself listening wistfully as he talked idly of the various jobs his men were engaged on, not daring to mention how she would loved to have gone and seen some of this action for herself. The cattle station aroused in her a consuming interest and curiosity, but Sloan made it quite clear he didn't want her there. He would never agree to showing her around, and she couldn't ask anyone else. All she could do was to try and enjoy what she could pick up in other ways.

As the meal progressed, Sloan's conversation dried up, and his face, as he watched Stacy, became increasingly grim. As his eyes travelled narrowly over her shining hair and pink mouth to her slender, strapped shoulders, she thought truculently that if he wouldn't let her leave he must learn to accept that her presence annoyed him. Yet although she tried not to look at him, there was such a longing inside her, she felt her eyes returning to him again and again. It didn't seem to matter that she got no encouragement.

Paula didn't help matters by saying, 'You were born on a farm, Stacy. I'm sure you would find a great deal to interest you on an outback cattle station. Why don't you take her around, Sloan?'

'I've already told you, Paula, there isn't much point.'

His eyes glinted, which ought to have warned Paula, but she rushed heedlessly on. 'You're not as busy as all that, dear. Why not let Stacy decide?'

Sloan's dark glance glittered, in a way Stacy found suddenly frightening as he swung around on her. He looked at her but he spoke to his mother, as though he had just come to a definite decision. 'I'm going to take Stacy to Cairns tomorrow. I don't see that it's necessary for her to stay any longer. I have a feeling she's more than a little homesick, and she won't get any better hanging around here.'

Frowning, Paula looked at Stacy's paling cheeks. In her shrewd glance was no little surprise. 'Are you really homesick, dear?'

This, Stacy supposed, was her cue to say yes. Almost she could feel Sloan willing her to. 'No!' she was startled to hear herself reply, as if not even Sloan could make her lie about this, 'I'm not homesick, but I—I do understand.'

'Which is more than I do!' Paula retorted coldly. 'The thought of home doesn't appear to be sending you into ecstasy, and I haven't yet decided,' she turned to Sloan, 'whether or not I'll stay in Australia. Since my illness,' she confessed, uncertainly, 'I just haven't been able to make my mind up what to do, so Stacy will just have to wait.'

'God!' Sloan exploded softly, 'women! Never to be hurried unless it suits them.'

'Not many of us have your capacity, Sloan, for knowing in an instant exactly the right thing to do,' Paula said frigidly.

'A pity,' he replied, with unsympathetic intolerance. Curtly he spoke to Stacy, his eyes boring into her, as if he would see her soul. 'Tell me, Miss Weldon, how do you intend filling your days, until my mother makes this momentous decision?'

Miserably Stacy stared down at her coffee, knowing he was stripping bare her every defence, and would go on attacking until he got rid of her. 'I'm not sure,' she said.

Before he could come back with another biting query, Paula leapt to her rescue. 'I don't see why you feel Stacy isn't pulling her weight, Sloan. After all, she hasn't been well herself lately, and just look at her! Even you must agree she still looks too pale. Mrs Turner thinks she needs building up, and when Mrs Turner is concerned for someone there's usually some justification.'

This time it was Stacy's turn to get in before Sloan could say anything. 'You're very kind, Mrs Maddison. And I appreciate your kindness, and Mrs Turner's, but I think perhaps Sloan is right. It would be better if I had something to do; the days do get long when I'm just hanging around, as he says. And I'm quite recovered, now, from my illness.'

'I bet you are,' Sloan returned, so cryptically that Paula looked alarmed.

''Sloan,' she smiled, his coldness driving her to speak on impulse, 'I don't think you need worry any more about Stacy having too little to do. I intend asking her to redecorate the master bedroom suite upstairs. You know it hasn't been touched since your father died. I suppose this was because we used the one I'm in now, at least after your father's leg injury made it almost impossible for him to climb the stairs. Anyway, it's years since the suite upstairs has been occupied and it certainly needs doing up. You wouldn't want to bring a bride to it as it is, and I'm sure she wouldn't want to start decorating as soon as you got back from your honeymoon.'

'Mother!' It was the first time Stacy had heard Sloan call his mother anything but Paula, and she jumped at the suppressed rage in his voice. As if Stacy didn't exist, he exclaimed, 'I won't have Miss Weldon nosing around up there.'

'But, Sloan,' Paula argued anxiously, 'when a man gets married, he must have everything right for his bride.'

His eyes went even colder. 'Women today have learnt not to expect so much.'

'Barbara might,' Paula dared.

Derisively his eyes met Stacy's widening ones, as if he recognised shock in the blue depth, and it pleased him. 'When I get married my bride won't be worrying immediately about colour schemes. When I allow her time to think about it, she can choose her own and I'll give the contract to a firm.'

'You forget,' Paula pressed stubbornly, 'that Stacy is an expert, too.' She flashed the girl a warm smile. 'Her mother told me much more than Stacy has done, and I've seen her work—not only at Thorn Farm,' she explained, 'we called one day on a friend of your mother's, dear, the one with a large house just through the village, and she showed me around. It's incredible what you achieved; the people were delighted. I'm sure Barbara...'

'That's enough, Paula!'

His voice was a whiplash, and Stacy didn't want Paula hurt. 'Mrs Maddison, I'd rather not.' Desperately she sought to convince Paula. 'A choice of colour can be a very personal thing, and very important, with most people.' She knew she must pretend she wasn't interested, nor was she. Even to think of doing rooms up for Sloan's bride was agony, and if she did undertake such an assignment she had no doubt Sloan would wring her neck. He was looking as though he could have done so in the spot.

Paula didn't appear to have heard what Stacy said, yet suddenly she looked inspired. 'Of course! We'll see Barbara at the dance. I can sound her out tactfully.'

'Mother!' now the anger leapt in Sloan's eyes. 'Mention

anything like that to her—or any woman—and I won't
be responsible!'

'Oh, well, I'm sorry, Sloan.'

'You can be.'

'I suppose,' Paula sighed, 'this is something a man of
your age likes to take care of himself. Come to think of it,
it was the present colour scheme which rather put me off
when I first came here, but your grandfather had had it
done in my honour and your father wouldn't hear tell of
it ever being changed.'

'I won't make that mistake,' Sloan said flatly, his eyes
resting mercilessly on Stacy's strained face.

The afternoon wore on, after he departed, and Paula,
complaining of a headache, said she would rest. It was warm
and while Stacy knew she could have spent a few pleasant
hours by the pool, she preferred to stay in her room nursing
her hurt, taking a kind of tortured pleasure in recalling the
complete coldness of the glance Sloan had cast in her direction, as he had risen from lunch and stalked out.

Stacy's room was pleasant, but after a while she found
it impossible to sit still any longer. Shudders began running through her, she could feel them beginning deep inside
her, and she had the horrible feeling she was about to break
down. Sloan had threatened before to send her away, but
after last night she had thought he meant to make her stay.
Now that he had openly discussed her departure with his
mother, Stacy was convinced he meant to be rid of her at
the first opportunity. Her supposed affair with Basil Bradley
was not to be overlooked or forgiven, and he wouldn't be
satisfied until she was gone.

Tearing off her dress, which she had thought such a
pretty shade of blue, she left it lying on the floor, in her
haste to find a pair of jeans and a cool shirt. She must try
to go somewhere. If only there had been a road along
which she might have escaped, but there wasn't. At
least...? Abruptly she halted on her way to the door, as if

she must stand still to work it out. Hadn't she noticed a road which ran a little distance from the creek? The station vehicles used it, mostly trucks and Land Rovers, but they seemed to go fairly well. Certainly they raised plenty of dust when a few of them set out together. Sometimes she'd wondered how those bringing up the rear were able to see? If she could find a truck which no one was using, couldn't she follow that road? She dared not ask for fear of arousing suspicion, but it must lead somewhere. Taronda could not be totally cut off from civilisation, apart from the air. Before planes were in use, they must have been able to get out, somehow, by road.

At the bottom of the stairs she regretted the few minutes she had lost when she bumped into Mrs Turner. 'I'm just going out for a while,' she said, trying not to look guilty.

'Do you good, dear,' Mrs Turner smiled at Stacy warmly, having grown fond of her. 'I'd have kept that nice dress on, though, if I'd been you. You young people, it's all jeans and that sort of thing these days.' Her sigh was followed by a sharper glance. 'Never mind, you go and get some nice fresh air, anyway. It's hot out, but it will do you no harm. You look as if you could do with it.'

Which wasn't exactly morale-boosting, but Stacy didn't much care what she looked like. Pushing her heavy hair from her eyes, she almost crept outside, hoping she wouldn't meet anyone else. If she hadn't seen Mrs Turner no one might have known she had left her room.

It was strangely exciting to steal around trying to find a truck of some kind, but it was also very nerve-racking. Taronda, however, might have been a ghost town that afternoon; there was no one about. The squat bungalows, the workshops, the store sheds and yards all seemed deserted. Even in the huts behind this compound, where the aboriginal workers and their families lived all appeared quiet.

The homestead, to many, would seem a grim, dry place, but the big sub-artesian bores kept it well supplied with water, allowing for some greenery, even in the dry.

Skirting two of the holding yards, Stacy came across a vehicle behind a low shed. Stopping dead in her tracks, she felt perspiration bead her brow as she glanced furtively around to make sure she was alone. She must be acting like a slippery baddy in a crime film, about to make off with the goods, she told herself mockingly. Yet that didn't stop her climbing into the truck as quickly as she could and jerking the door shut behind her. Then came what seemed the greatest miracle of the lot—the keys were still in the ignition. Switching it on, she released the brake, reversing towards the creek. If anyone saw the truck leaving she hoped they would believe it was just one of the men.

Stacy had often thought how good it would be to be able to explore, but she had never dreamt the sense of freedom would make her feel as good as this. The gas gauge said half full and she would be there and back before Sloan ever found out she was gone. She didn't intend going far; maybe ten or twenty miles, it all depended what took her fancy, and if she stuck close by the truck she surely couldn't go wrong.

Having asked Paula, Stacy knew that unsealed roads could soon become a quagmire in the wet, from November to March, and that even the bitumen roads were constantly cut off by creeks overflowing over them during the same period, but she didn't think she would be in danger from anything like that today. The track she followed through the scrub was clearly marked and hard, if it did seem to disappear in places.

Driving with a fair amount of confidence, she thought how good it was to have something else to concentrate on, other than her own unsolvable problems. Pressing on through tracts of open grasslands, she hit stretches where the ground was red and looked well grazed. There were tall gum trees by the creeks, then patches of wooded savannah and stunted eucalypts. In these areas, where she sometimes caught glimpses of glistening water, flocks of birds flew up before her, their gaudily coloured plumes glinting in the sun, unknown species but so attractive she vowed to ask Paula about them.

Apart from the birds, she enjoyed the clear stretches best, where the wind blew wild and free over the great plains, and the grasslands rolled away to wide, bluish horizons. She could see no cattle or horses, certainly no sign of men with other trucks or forms of transport, but the isolation and loneliness of the terrain excited rather than frightened her and she imagined this was how the first explorers must have seen it, all those years ago.

Yet this didn't make her unaware of the dangers which might be lurking behind such a scale of grandeur. The patches of what she took to be swampy ground worried her a little, instinctively, and it was on one of these stretches that disaster struck. She had covered about fifteen miles and was just thinking of turning back when she hit the kangaroo. Afterwards she had no clear recollection of what happened. She hadn't been going very fast when she saw one dash from the bush. This one she managed to avoid, but she hadn't spotted its mate soon enough. With great hops the six-foot-tall animal, following behind, had crashed straight into her. Frantically, at the last minute, she had torn the wheel around, but in doing so had driven right into a huge snow gum. For a while she just stared blankly through the windscreen at the dead animal. With great presence of mind she switched off the engine, yet was scarcely aware of her hand moving.

How long she sat there feeling completely shaken, she never knew. She thought she must have caught her shoulder as the lurching vehicle came to an abrupt stop, but she almost welcomed the pain as it took a little of her attention

away from the poor kangaroo, and the ache in her heart.
Many thousands of kangaroos were killed on the highways
each year, but this didn't make her feel any better about a
death she considered herself solely responsible for. The
kangaroos might do untold damage to crops, but she could
only think how a few moments ago this one had been alive
and enjoying itself.

At last, making a great effort, she got out of the truck.
She had been considering doing this before she had hit
the kangaroo, but now she had no other option as she
couldn't see the truck moving again in a hurry; it was
wedged too firmly against the tree. On the ground she stood
still for a minute, flexing her shoulder. It seemed all right,
she could move it. There might be some bruising, but
nothing must be broken. The truck, she saw unhappily,
would not be so easily put right. The front end of it lurched
at a dreadful angle, with one wheel nearly buried in what
looked like soft sand. She shuddered to think of what Sloan
was going to say.

Very soon she would try and do something about it, but
first she must get herself pulled together. Her head was
beginning to ache and her throat felt dry. She felt parched
and terribly angry that she hadn't thought to bring any
water. She had made, was still making, one mistake after
another, it seemed. Hopefully, averting her eyes from the
dead kangaroo, she looked around. There must be a creek
somewhere near. The wet hadn't been over that long; they
couldn't all have dried up.

Half an hour later she was still telling herself it must be
possible to find water somewhere.

Another flock of colourful birds flew up as she hopefully
approached a creek with a thickly wooded appearance.
Unfortunately that was all it was—thick, big scrub and
undergrowth, which Stacy fancied might hide innumerable
snakes. Skirting this, she went on, quite aware of what she
was doing; it wasn't as if she had hit her head or anything.

She was merely looking for a drink, and had no intention of getting lost.

Eventually she did find a creek with a little water left in it, and sat drinking and washing her hot face and hands. The water was warm and tasted a bit peculiar, but it was wet and very welcome. This, and the silence, soothed her jumping nerves so much, she kept dozing off from time to time.

Once, as she slept, she fancied she heard the drone of a plane, but such a familiar sound made little impact. It was strange, in a way, how everyone out here seemed so used to this kind of transport. Even the aborigine stockmen loved flying, for all they still went walkabout. Sloan had mentioned, at lunch, that two of his best men had taken their wives and gone off into the bush. They would come back, he had said, when Stacy asked, but it could be weeks. The old tribal customs, however, were recognised and respected. In a week or two he would check up on them to see if they were all right as one of the men was getting old. If necessary he would drop off some food.

So much care and concern for everyone, Stacy mused, for everyone, that was, but a promiscuous little English girl. Sloan Maddison ran Taronda like a small kingdom, with all the tolerance in the world for loyal subjects but none whatsoever for those whom he considered had stepped out of line.

A light wind blew up, warm but utterly desolate, with its overtones of wild, haunting loneliness. Opening her eyes, Stacy saw an eagle hovering above her, its great wings spread. As she watched it came close, its cruel beak parting as though in anticipation of her tender young limbs. Startled out of her stupor, she stood up, waving her arms. This appeared to frighten it off, but as it went she soon discovered what had really scared it.

Like another eagle, but with infinitely more noise, the helicopter reared over the creek, rising as if from nowhere, the largest bird of prey of them all. It must have seen something as the pilot steadied to hover, poised even more dramatically than the eagle. When it suddenly disappeared again behind the trees, Stacy felt no relief, as she suspected it was coming down.

With a frown of introspection on her tired face, she stared unseeingly at the ground, concentrating wholly on listening. Yes, she was sure of it. Nothing could cut off so dramatically and still remain in the air for so long without restarting.

She moved quickly, now, not wanting to be found, if it was someone looking for her, until she had righted the truck. Without over-much care she dived straight into the undergrowth, only to come bang up against Sloan. 'Oh!' she gasped, her eyes so frightened in her pale face he could have been the devil. 'Fancy meeting you!'

'And what do I say?' Viciously he grabbed hold of her flying body. 'What a pleasant surprise! Will that do? Just as if we were meeting in Queen Street, Brisbane.' His voice went cold, with a kind of restrained violence as he saw her shocked face. 'What the hell did you think you were playing at, you little fool?'

'No need to be so—so—like that!' she stuttered, the tightness in her throat causing her to speak aggressively. Only by doing it this way could she hope to suppress the desire to fall into his arms, to cling desperately to his dusty shirt and weep.

He held her by the shoulders and she wished she could escape him, as his hands seemed to reflect the brutality of his feelings. She could see he was in a ferocious rage, not choosing his words at all carefully. There was a whiteness about his mouth, which was drawn in one hard, straight line. 'So what?' he rasped grimly. 'How do you think I felt when it was discovered you'd gone!'

'How would I know?' The agonising pain of heartache still forced a note of infuriating carelessness. 'I've never had free access to your feelings. If I'd died out here you might have been glad to have got rid of me. I don't even know what you intend doing now.'

'Right now I could beat the living daylights out of you, so go easy, Stacy. What made you run away?'

'I'm not running away!' She wasn't aware of the tears which began running down her face, but she did know she was trembling too hard to be able to speak clearly. 'You call me a fool, but I'm not such a fool as to not realise I wouldn't get far if I did that!'

'Then what in heaven's name were you up to?'

At a loss for words, Stacy stared at him. It suddenly came to her that she had never seen him looking so dishevelled, not even when his mother had taken ill. His hair was rumpled, his shirt torn and red dust clung to his skin. He had been helping with the mustering and must have come straight after her without washing, but it was his expression of rough, primitive urgency which she found most frightening. 'I was only trying to take a look around,' she replied at last. 'There was no one I could ask, and I did want to see something of the station before I left.'

'I could shake you!' His voice was still thick with anger. 'What happened? Come on, out with it. I found the truck. What hit you? I suppose it was the dead kangaroo?'

Bleakly, as visions of it and the wrecked truck rushed up on her, she closed her eyes. 'Yes. It just hopped out on me...'

For a brief moment he said nothing, but opening her eyes she saw his blazing with anger. 'You realise you could have been killed? And not only that, you committed the most foolish crime of the lot, wandering off into the bush."

Indifferently she shrugged, wondering why it mattered. 'I don't know what all the fuss is about.' She rubbed the back of her hand carelessly across her damp eyes. 'I was thirsty and just went to find a drink of water before beginning to walk home.' She didn't try to pretend she had really expected to get the truck out.

In view of her strained face, perhaps, Sloan seemed to

change his mind about rating her further. If his eyes still smouldered, he put a greater guard on his tongue as he watched her closely for several long seconds. 'I gather you weren't going too hard when that 'roo hit you, but you must have got a fright. Do you feel all right?'

No, she wanted to shout at him, I feel terrible, and it's all your fault. Instead she said, 'Yes,' very calmly, only the faintest of tremors in her voice.

Again there was a slight hesitation before his mouth clamped. 'I'll have you home in a few minutes, then I'll contact the men. All the available staff are out looking for you.'

This would be another black mark against her. 'Who told you I'd gone? Mrs Turner?'

'No. The stockman, whose truck you took, but it took time to locate me.'

'You shouldn't have bothered.'

'I've been out of my mind!' he said harshly.

Dully, Stacy supposed he would have been, no matter who had been lost. 'I'm sorry,' she whispered.

'Come on, Stacy.' Suddenly impatient, he turned her the way he had come. 'You may not believe it, but you're about three miles from the truck. That I found you at all was a miracle.'

It was peculiar, but when she tried to walk she did nothing but stumble. Not even the brandy Sloan forced her to drink from a small flask he carried helped much. With a sigh he picked her up and carried her the rest of the way, her face pressed against his torn shirt, her protests stifled on the warm, hair-roughened skin of his broad chest. After a few minutes she put her two arms around him and clung, not really caring what he thought. Drowsy with brandy, she pressed closer, letting a hot, sweet surge of desire take over, marvelling at the way it eliminated lesser things.

Unfortunately, she had to face reality again, once they reached the truck. Sloan took her there in the helicopter, which was only about half a mile away from where he had found her. He would have gone straight back to the homestead if he hadn't forgotten to take the keys from the ignition and check one or two other things.

Stacy hadn't realised how damaged the truck was and gazed at it with dismay. 'You'll have to let me pay,' she said.

'Maybe I will,' he agreed shortly, 'but we won't go into that now. I just want the keys, although,' he added drily, 'I don't think anyone's likely to try and steal it, or that they would get far if they did.'

As they took off again Stacy did wonder why he hadn't thought of that when he had been here before. Usually he never overlooked a thing.

'You're lucky to have got off with a sore shoulder,' he said bluntly. 'I'll take a look at it later. Is it still sore?'

'Not too bad,' she answered. It wasn't, and she found herself wishing she hadn't mentioned it, having no wish to have Sloan poking around. 'I'll have a hot bath. That usually cures everything.'

'It could be dangerous to think so.' He threw her a searching glance as the helicopter levelled out on the cooling air. She noticed their shadow on the ground lengthening and became aware that she must have slept longer than she'd thought at the creek. 'I didn't mean to go to sleep. I was looking for water,' she explained, as if by way of apology.

'I don't imagine you did,' he said curtly, 'but you'd had a fright and were probably struggling with other problems as well as shock. That's when sleep often takes over. It's a kind of defence mechanism against the unanswerable.'

'Who would have dreamt you were so clever,' she whispered fiercely, 'as well as everything else!'

The angle of his chin hardened. 'Well, just you lie back while I work that one out, Miss Weldon. By the time I have, we should be home.'

Stacy had no trouble at the homestead. Sloan put the

helicopter down on the wide lawns in front of the house,
something which Paula told her afterwards she had never
known him do before, so she had just a few steps to walk
to the house. Grimly Sloan supervised, of course, but Stacy
found she wasn't hurt so much as shaken, and she was used
to Sloan's disapproval. Since coming here she had known
little else.

Paula's headache had taken a long time to clear, and
when it did she had decided to stay in bed. As no one had
mentioned that Stacy was missing, Sloan advised Stacy to
look in on her later, if she felt up to it, but that it might
be better to leave it until morning. There didn't seem
much point in upsetting his mother unnecessarily.

Mrs Turner was inclined to fuss but also managed to
look reproachful, as if she privately considered Stacy
should have known better than to alarm the whole station.
It was only when she noticed Stacy's air of undoubted
strain that her kind heart took over and she relented, declaring it could happen to anybody.

'Not anybody,' Sloan corrected, any hint of compassion
obviously fading. 'There are still those, thank God, with
more sense.'

'I'm sure Stacy is willing to learn,' Mrs Turner reproved
him tartly, as she went to run Stacy's bath. 'And I can look
after her now.' Her expression said quite plainly there
was no need for him to stay in the bedroom any longer.

'You get round them all, don't you?' he taunted, letting
go of the arm by which he had helped her upstairs. 'One
pathetic little glance and you have them eating out of your
hand.'

'If you mean Mrs Turner, she's just naturally kind,'
Stacy faltered. 'I expect she would do the same for anyone,
just as you've done yourself this afternoon.' Taking no
notice of his quick frown, she rushed on, 'I'm sorry for all
the trouble I've caused, Sloan, and I'd like to thank you.
I really am grateful. I . . .'

'Save it, will you,' he growled. 'It was nothing personal, so don't go getting ideas.' Swinging on his heel, he added curtly, 'I'd get into that bath as fast as you can, if I were you. I'll come back after you've had it and take a look at your shoulder.'

She had hoped to be out of the bath and dressed long before he returned, but when she came from the bathroom he was standing looking out of her bedroom window.

Drawing her negligé closer around her, she was conscious of her clean-washed face, her hair tumbling uncombed down her back. Quickly she tossed it out of her eyes as he turned and came towards her. 'My shoulder is fine,' she assured him nervously. 'Just a little bruising.'

'I have to see it.' His eyes narrowed on her mutinous face. 'Come on, Stacy! Stop prevaricating like some chaste young maiden. Mrs Turner's busy getting you something light on a tray. Like Paula, you'll be better in bed, even if it's going to seem like having a house full of invalids.'

Stacy shrank, seeing only his intolerance. 'But there's no need! I'm certainly not ill, or anything like it. And,' her voice broke on an anguished note of indignation, 'I don't see what my being chaste, or anything else, has to do with it!'

He stared at her, a cold smile on his firm mouth. 'Don't you? You can't be so dumb that I have to explain? I imagine you were quite used to showing Basil Bradley much more than one bare shoulder!'

She was shaking at his grim tones. 'Please, Sloan, don't!' Tonight she didn't feel up to his cold cynicism. All she really wanted was a little warmth, but if she couldn't have that she might have hoped to have been spared more of his contempt. Seeking to end the matter as quickly as possible, she pushed the edge of the negligé from off her right shoulder, keeping the front of it tightly closed with her other hand. 'There,' she whispered, 'see what you like.'

His mouth twisted with faint amusement, but he was

surprisingly gentle, his expert probing arousing sensations worse to bear than pain. She could see he had taken a quick shower, and the clean, masculine scent of his body seemed to draw her like a magnet. He only touched her shoulder, but suddenly she wanted much more than that. He was so near, so dear to her! Helplessly she drew a long, trembling breath and closed her eyes, her whole body longing to melt into his. As she stared helplessly at his dark, bent head, her fingers slackened unconsciously on the front of her negligé.

'Stacy!' He spoke through his teeth as he stared down at the pale skin exposed to his view. His voice thickened, as one of her hands reached out to him. 'Stacy, do you realise what you're doing?'

But Mrs Turner was there with Stacy's dinner, bumping clumsily against the door as she tried to open it without putting the tray down.

'Wait a minute, I'm coming,' Sloan called curtly, savagely thrusting aside Stacy's clinging fingers.

As Mrs Turner passed him in the doorway with a murmur of thanks, he said, 'I don't think we need bother the Flying Doc about Stacy's shoulder. There's nothing much wrong with it, as far as I can see, and it certainly doesn't appear to be restricting her in any way.'

On that note of sarcasm he departed, leaving Stacy to hide her flushed face as best she could. She thanked Mrs. Turner for her dinner. 'I could have come down, you know,' she said tonelessly. 'Sloan shouldn't have insisted I have it up here. You have enough to do.'

'Well, he usually knows best.' Mrs Turner looked pleased at Stacy's few words of appreciation. 'And he's used to coping with accidents. The Flying Doctor service relies a lot on the good judgment of station owners and their staff. You can depend on it if there'd been any likelihood of serious injury, Sloan would have had them out immediately. As it is, it's sometimes enough just to speak to them over the air and have their advice.'

The light meal Mrs Turner had prepared was delicious, but Stacy found she could scarcely eat it. She felt too sick with embarrassment, remembering the way she had practically begged for Sloan's caresses. What, she wondered, might have happened if Mrs Turner hadn't arrived?

Pushing her tray aside, she drank the hot tea Mrs Turner had provided instead of coffee. For the first time she was conscious of how strong physical feelings might overcome everything else, and the knowledge depressed her. Combined with her love for Sloan, this could reduce her defences to a minimum. It made her realise just how vulnerable she might be if he were to guess her weakness and take advantage of it.

CHAPTER NINE

AFTER finishing all she could manage Stacy picked up her tray and carried it downstairs. Mrs Turner was nowhere to be seen, so after washing her dishes Stacy decided she might as well go back to bed. As Mrs Maddison was apparently sleeping there didn't seem much point in looking in on her. Tomorrow she would see her and try to explain everything.

Back in her bedroom, Stacy tried to sleep, but couldn't. The hours dragged. It must have been all those cat-naps during the afternoon beside the creek, but now she didn't feel at all sleepy. Perhaps she might have been wiser to have gone out for a walk in the garden, after she had taken her tray down. Hopefully she glanced towards the window. It didn't seem a very dark night. Maybe even now she could slip outside. Even the thought of those cool, dark arbours acted like magic on her overheated skin.

Without putting on a light, she slipped from her bed. Unfortunately, on her way to the window she stumbled against the chair she had pulled out to place her tray on, and it crashed loudly against the dressing table.

A little startled but not unduly alarmed, she was groping to pick it up when the door was thrown open.

'What on earth's going on in here?' Sloan's voice came cracking through the darkness the instant before he switched on the light.

Blinded by the sudden brightness, Stacy flung a hand across her eyes. 'It's quite all right, I only knocked over a chair.'

'Knocked over a chair? God, I thought it was the house coming down!' Slamming the door formidably behind him he strode over to her. 'I hadn't quite got into bed, but even if I had I would have had to investigate.'

'Point taken,' Stacy managed tersely.

'If that's supposed to express appreciation,' he snapped, 'you'd better try again. If there's one thing I could do with it's a good night's sleep.'

'I—I'm sorry I disturbed you.' Stacy's eyes, sliding to him with a will of their own, discovered he wore nothing but a pair of pants, belted tightly to his firm waist. Conscious of her thin negligé, which she still wore as she had only been lying on top of her bed, she looked quickly away from him.

'Disturb me!' he laughed harshly. 'You've been doing that, Stacy, ever since I met you, on and off. What the hell were you up to, tripping over in the dark? You have a bed-light.'

'I thought of taking a walk.' Her throat was dry and she was silently praying he would go. She had never seen Sloan like this before and the naked breadth of his shoulders slightly stunned her. Slowly her eyes moved over him, caution momentarily forgotten as sensuous pleasure took its place. His muscles were firm and strong under warm, tanned skin, which in turn was covered by a wealth of fine, dark hair, continuing down past his navel. His waist tapered slightly, but his thighs were powerful, their strength very apparent as he towered above her.

'I wanted to go for a walk,' she breathed, as if desperately trying to convince herself she still did, and there was something oddly defenceless in the way she put her hands to her face and closed her eyes.

'Stacy!'

The coldness in his voice shook her, as it so often did, but it also jerked her upright and brought her eyes to his face. 'I've told you, there's nothing to worry about,' she gasped. 'You can leave me.'

'Do you want me to?' He came nearer. 'How do you

usually talk to a man when he comes to your bedroom?'

'I—don't.'

'Passion without words, huh?' He took no account of her bemused state as his arms went out to take hold of her.

It was no use trying to move. She couldn't, and there was a kind of helpless fascination in watching him push her robe aside, slowly but deliberately, as he bent his dark head.

Involuntarily she flinched, then swayed towards him, almost as she had done a few hours ago. A dizzying feeling swept over her, and her heart began to race as he placed his mouth against the visible movement of it under her white skin.

'You're beautiful,' he murmured thickly, with sudden urgency, his arms sliding around her back, his hands pressing her to him.

Pliantly she lay against him, until the gentle brushing of his mouth threatened to send her almost crazy. Sloan had made love to women before—he was no novice in the fine art of arousal. The pressures he was subjecting her to were way out of Stacy's experience, but her body was more sensuous than she had ever suspected. Rapidly she found herself responding to him, her fingers curving fiercely on his broad shoulders, locking tightly at the back of his neck.

It was then that he lifted his head to look at her, seeming to have no remorse that the light shining down on her illuminated each separate feature, the piercing tension in her body, the feverish desire on her face. She knew she should be trying to fight him, but she was also hazily aware how time was running out for her. In another few days she would be gone and might never see him again. She felt his hands sliding downwards, pausing below her waist to crush her closer, making her conscious, with his breathing unsteady on her cheek, of how much he wanted her.

Then, when she groaned, his mouth took her own and she was shuddering under the flaming warmth of his kiss. As his lips plundered hers, the buckle of his belt bit hard into her soft stomach and impatiently he ripped it off. The hard driving force of him overwhelmed her, as his lips found her breasts before coming back to her mouth, and every bit of her resistance collapsed. It was like standing on a seashore, being hit by wave after wave of hot desire. There was no end to it. It flooded every inch of her, invading every secret part until she was totally enveloped in exquisite pain. Her bones seemed to melt, her body went limp, wholly yielding to the urgency and passion of his. Very slightly he raised his mouth, on the verge of taking her.

'I love you,' she gasped, barely aware of what she was saying but finding nothing else which would express so completely her feelings. She was only conscious of an unbearable compunction to surrender everything, even her thoughts. 'I love you,' she whispered again, thrusting slender fingers cravingly through his thick hair.

'No!' Suddenly, his face hardening, he picked her up and deposited her roughly on to the bed. But instead of joining her there, he detached her clinging arms and stepped back.

'Sloan?' She was breathing deeply, her blue eyes dilated with the force of her emotions, blurred and pleading. 'Where are you going?'

'Going, Stacy? Need you ask?' His voice was so curt she shrank instinctively. 'Are you asking me to stay and make love to you, an innocent young girl? If I did that in this house, I might never get you out of it.'

The exact context of his words escaped her. 'I love you, Sloan,' she muttered frantically, as though she must keep on repeating it.

'No, you don't!' He looked as though he could have slapped her. 'Never mix love with this kind of thing, Stacy, it's no answer. One can be a kind of insult without the other. Or didn't you realise?'

Her mind not up to grappling with this, she stared up at him, her face full of a most desperate anguish which never seemed to reach him.

Completely in control now, his eyes fixed on her face dispassionately. 'Goodnight,' he said, and without another word, turned to switch off the light and close the door.

Outside came the plaintive moan of the night wind bringing with it the utter desolation of the lonely plains. Burying her hot face in her pillow, Stacy sobbed, acknowledging the death of hope, once and for all.

It might have been over-dramatic, but the hopelessness of the situation stayed with her all the next day, and though nice things happened which brought happiness to other people on the station, she found her heart too heavy to share in their pleasure.

Paula, quite recovered, was in a good mood, which improved even more when Sloan brought a message from Sally saying that Bill was bringing her and the children from Brisbane for the party on the following night. They were due to arrive at Taronda early that afternoon.

'Such a mysterious girl!' Paula exclaimed. 'What are she and Bill doing in Brisbane, of all places?'

'What Sally's been doing ever since I can remember,' Sloan answered dryly. 'Making as big a mystery as possible out of her life. She intends you should wonder, until you're half mad with curiosity. I should just wait until she arrives.'

'There's nothing else I can do,' Paula sighed. 'But it's going to be lovely to have them. Did she say how long they'd be able to stay?' As Sloan shook his head on an impatient sigh, she turned to Stacy. 'Have you a moment, dear, to go and tell Mrs Turner I want to see her?'

Stacy, glad of any excuse to leave the room, with Sloan in it, went immediately. Feeling her pulse racing because of his nearness, she deeply regretted her confession of love. Her only consolation was that he hadn't believed her.

In the kitchen, Mrs Turner said, 'If it's to tell me Sally is coming, I already know. You can tell Mrs Maddison I'm on my way to make up their beds.'

Stacy smiled ruefully. Mrs Turner had ears all round

her head, nothing escaped her. 'I think she wanted to tell you herself.'

'Yes, well,' Mrs Turner relented, 'I'd better look in.'

Later, Stacy helped Mrs Turner with the beds, and was delighted when the housekeeper allowed her to do several more smaller jobs before she was dismissed to arrange the flowers for Paula. Here all Stacy's wonderful colour sense came into its own, and the result was really impressive. In the hustle and bustle, her unfortunate adventures of the day before were almost overlooked, and she was glad. To be reminded of any part of it was a torment she would rather be spared.

The visitors arrived in time for lunch, Sloan having driven out to meet them on the air-strip. Sally was exuberant, with Bill and the children in excellent spirits. Lunch was served immediately by a beaming Mrs Turner and a smiling Aborigine girl, and Sally exclaimed with delight over the flowers.

'Stacy did them for me,' Paula smiled.

'Oh, how clever!' Generous in her praise, Sally looked wryly at Stacy. 'Why can I never manage to get mine to look like this? You'll have to show me.'

'She's a very clever girl, in more ways than one,' Sloan mocked cynically.

'Are you two still at loggerheads?' Sally laughed, catching the atmosphere shrewdly, but deciding to make light of it.

Sloan, however, caught on sharply. 'Did Miss Weldon give you this impression in Sydney?'

If Sally's eyes flew, wide open, to her brother's disparaging face, she otherwise refrained from expressing her surprised curiosity. 'No, darling,' she teased, half jokingly, which was the most she ever dared with Sloan. 'It was more your own tone, that day you rang.'

There was an uncomfortable little silence, during which Bill made use of the opportunity to announce that Sally and he were coming to live in Brisbane. In fact his firm had already moved him there to open and take charge of a new branch.

'We didn't want to tell you until we were sure it was all settled, Mother,' Sally took over from Bill, 'but now I think we can safely say we'll be there until Bill retires. Won't we, darling?'

Paula was overwhelmed, Stacy could see. 'Why, you'll be practically on Taronda's doorstep!'

Stacy couldn't prevent a wry smile, as she wondered if she could ever learn to consider great distances as these people did. Queensland alone—named by Queen Victoria—was, as Sloan had told her, over seven times the size of England. And Sally, in Brisbane, would be at one end while Taronda, here in the Gulf country, was practically at the other. To many Australians this would be a gentle hop!

Sally, who had always missed her mother, said hopefully, 'There's a wonderful little house not far from us with terrific views. You would love it, Mother. It's very countrified and several of your friends live near.'

Looking startled, then intrigued, her face a study of several emotions, Paula stared at her daughter, Mrs Turner's beautifully done steak almost forgotten. 'And I suppose I would be near my grandchildren.' Her face glowed.

'They'd love to have you—we all would!'

What about Bilton Manor? Stacy wanted to cry, but catching Sloan's eye was immediately silenced. As if he had spoken, he told her Paula must make up her own mind, without interference. Anyway, Stacy subsided, it wasn't her place.

Paula sighed, glancing at Stacy apologetically. 'I'd almost decided to go back to England, to spend my last years there. Then came this operation and I had a sudden yearning for Australia. I think it must have been devised by fate to show me where my heart really lay. My duty, too, must be here, looking after Sloan.' Anxiously she turned to him. 'What do you think of this new idea, Sloan? You weren't keen for me to settle in England, but this would mean leaving you just the same.'

His face was impassive. 'I raise no objections to Brisbane, Paula. If I marry, Brisbane would make sense. The U.K., for you, is too far away.'

'Is Barbara coming to Jill's party?' Sally asked, her regrettable impulsiveness rewarded by a chilly stare from her brother.

'What's more to the point,' he admonished her, 'is getting your mother sensibly settled. Then you can feel free to speculate on something else.'

As if determined to follow his advice to the letter, Paula spent most of that day and much of the following discussing it with Sally and Bill, while Stacy kept the children out of the way. This was no hardship as she loved children and Sally's two were really darlings. She took them for long walks and played with them at the nearest creek. They could have stayed in the garden by the pool, but Stacy decided they should take advantage of the wonderful freedom Taronda offered. A pool could be found anywhere, but not Taronda. If anything, she was grateful the children were there as it helped keep her mind off Sloan and his apparent determination to take a wife.

He rode past the next morning when she was out with them. Bill junior had run on, his sister following, when Sloan paused beside Stacy. 'Having fun?' from the back of his great horse, his eyes were mocking yet intent as they lingered on her long, slim legs clad only in an old pair of Sally's shorts. 'Don't the children bother you?'

'I like children, they're no bother.'

'Planning some of your own?'

Her bright head dropped. She couldn't tell him this was out for her now. 'I wouldn't have minded a couple,' she said despondently.

'But not before you'd had your fun, I suppose. You'd want to be at least thirty, and every one of them planned. No mad, irresponsible interludes where anything might happen?'

Her pulses throbbing she flung away from him, driven indiscreetly from her hard held calm by his cool taunts. 'If I were married,' she cried, 'I would want children straight away. Why should I want to wait until I was thirty?'

'Why, indeed?' he drawled, riding on.

Feeling ashamed, but unable to think of anything else, she tried to use the children as an excuse to get out of going to the party. Finding Paula and Sally together in the drawing room after tea, she began abruptly, 'I think I've been out in the sun too long, Mrs Maddison. My head is beginning to ache rather badly. I really believe I'd be wiser to stay at home this evening.'

Sloan spoke behind her with a firmness which made her jump. 'Go and get dressed, Stacy. Have a hot bath first, which will help, and I'll bring you something for your head. Sally,' his eyes were cold as he glanced at his sister, 'couldn't you have seen to your own two kids for at least a while this afternoon? I love them, but I'm not too fond of the way you're letting them wear Stacy out.'

'Oh, please!' Stacy intervened, ready to sink through the floor, her voice reduced to a peculiar hoarse whisper. How could she not have seen him standing just outside the verandah doors! 'No one would notice if I wasn't at the party, as no one knows me.'

'Something which will soon be remedied,' he rejoined smoothly. 'You're going, Stacy, be in no doubt about that, if I have to take you there by force.'

'Really, Sloan!' Paula demurred, while Sally stood by, startled out of her usual neat and conventional way of thinking. 'Really Sloan,' Paula tried again, 'do you have to speak to Stacy like this? I would certainly like her with us at Jill's party. For one thing, I would appreciate her help, but if she feels ill. . . '

'Stacy!'

Sloan only said her name, but Stacy felt defeated. 'All right, I'll go,' she capitulated nervously, finding nothing she could argue with successfully in the remote coldness of his face. Frustrated, she bit her lip, giving in with as much good grace as she could find. She could be angry with him, shout at him, cry, argue and defy him, but in the end it all boiled down to the one thing—she obeyed him!

On her way upstairs she couldn't resist looking into the kitchen, where the children were enjoying their eggs and milk before going to bed. Mrs Turner was to be left in charge of them and there was plenty of other staff.

'You're darlings,' Stacy smiled, when they demanded a hug before she went.

'I can see you like them, anyway,' Mrs Turner conceded wryly, knowing from experience that they could be proper limbs of mischief. 'And they obviously like you.' Her wide, indulgent smile rather spoilt the sternness of her next words. 'The trouble is we all spoil them when they come here, when what they really need is a firm hand.'

'As does someone else, Mrs Turner!'

Stacy gasped, took one look at Sloan, who must have followed her, and fled.

Her bath was hot and, as he had suggested, it did make her feel better, but she almost fell asleep in it. Consequently, although she managed to complete her hair and make-up, she was just putting on her dress when he walked in with a glass of water and two tablets. He didn't knock and she stopped fumbling with her zip to stare at him. Then, for a heart-stopping moment, she had to close her eyes and see him as a tyrannical husband, commanding, urging, persuading, managing to make her do exactly as he wanted because of the sheer force of her love for him. A love which might make her weakly submissive, whatever he demanded. If only he had been even a little in need of her! If he hadn't had a penny, had been ill, in need of sympathy and help, would she have stood a chance? He treated her with contempt, made no bones about what he thought of her past record, yet sometimes, the way he spoke, the way he looked at her ...?

'Stacy!' It seemed he must always be speaking her name with a marked degree of exasperation. Putting down the glass he carried, he twisted her around, zipping up her dress in a way which opened Stacy's eyes in alarm, making her shudder to imagine what might have happened to any skin which had been caught. But no skin was caught, miraculously she was unscathed, as far as her flesh was concerned. Her nerves were another thing. Where had he learnt such expertise? With Barbara Bolam?

Carefully, with shaking fingers, she adjusted the fine, floating panels of silky chiffon which was all the dress was composed of. It was slightly see-through but not terribly daring. Unless one looked closely it was as demure as anyone could wish for. In it Stacy's tender young beauty became vividly arresting, something which brought an unreadable expression to Sloan's face.

Picking up the glass again, he passed her the tablets, watching as she obediently swallowed them. 'You can take that dazed look off your face,' he snapped intolerantly. 'We're late as it is. Aspirins might cure a head, but daydreams are another thing.'

'I wasn't daydreaming!' She took another quick drink, giving him back the glass while she reached for her high-heeled silver sandals. The straps around her ankles were awkward to fasten, but helped keep her mind off the last time Sloan had been in her room.

With a sigh he bent down, pushing her fumbling fingers aside to complete the job himself, then grimly surveying her arched, silver-clad foot. 'What's so attractive about a slender foot on an impractical heel?' he demanded.

'Don't you approve?' She tried to speak evenly, but his hand was still around her ankle, his touch shooting flames up her limbs. A shudder affected her strangely, running, as it did, right through her. Feverishly she hoped he wouldn't notice, as he straightened.

He did, and his eyes narrowed apprehendingly as they travelled slowly up her tremulous young figure, to judge astutely the unconscious, pleading softness of her lips. With a wariness born of experience his intent gaze left her for one uncontrollable instant, to flick to the bed. Able to assess the depth of her frustrated desire better than Stacy, he looked at her mouth again, his own enigmatically hardening with the hold he kept over himself. Stacy's face went pale as she swayed and drew suddenly away from him, feeling shamefully startled, beyond words, by the force of her own emotions.

'Don't worry.' His rising desire was immediately curbed, so Stacy felt she had merely imagined it. The faint redness on his cheekbones faded as he mocked, 'We haven't time, and you'd need a lot of that, wouldn't you? You're very young, Stacy, full of half-fledged responses, which might satisfy the Basil Bradleys of this world, but never me.'

Stacy tried to look away from him, and when he wouldn't allow it, she hoped her sense of inadequacy didn't show. 'I wouldn't,' she stuttered, 'even begin to try!'

'You'd have to grow up first, my dear. No man enjoys wiping up tears.'

'I can do without your advice, although how you do love dishing it out.' Audibly, her breath dragged. 'I imagine Barbara Bolam satisfies you in every way? You won't remember her last tears.'

'I won't answer that.' His dark face was instantly formidable, but Stacy rushed on, with a reckless disregard for danger.

'I suppose a gentleman never tells?'

Never had she thought to see him so ready to lay her

over his knee. It could only have been a regard for the late-
ness of the hour which stopped him. With commendable
control he turned to pick up her light wrap, to drop it firmly
around her tense shoulders.

'The others will be waiting.' He ignored her last remark
as if it didn't deserve an answer. 'And Stacy—?'

'Yes?'

'Try and behave yourself.'

'How do you mean?' With a jerk she pulled from his
grasp, as his dark eyes rested coldly on her, all the warmth
long gone from them.

'You know quite well what I mean.'

He mightn't like her, but should that make him so hard
and unforgiving, so unwilling to believe she could ever be
the first Stacy he had known? She felt slightly sick. 'You—
you're talking about other men?'

'I am.'

'I see.' Against his measured tones she found no defence,
but the desire to continue fighting him seemed to fade. He
would never trust her again, so why waste her time? Forcing
her unhappiness into a lighter, careless mood, she smiled
coolly, almost as though she was considering a compliment,
rather than an insult. 'I promise I won't do anything to
embarrass your family, Sloan. Anyway, I don't suppose I'll
attract very much attention. Your mother says there'll be
dozens of pretty girls there tonight, so I expect the competi-
tion will be fierce. Will you know them all?'

'Most,' he replied dryly.

She nodded painfully, and moved in front of him out of
the room.

They travelled to Jill's party in Sloan's larger plane,
which took the five of them nicely. Paula was in the best of
moods and Stacy suspected it was based on relief, from
having come to a definite decision regarding her future. It
was quite clear to Stacy that Paula would go to live near
Sally, in Brisbane. No one said anything, but Stacy felt sure.

She also had a feeling that Paula might ask her to go with her to Brisbane, to help decorate this new house, but if this happened she knew she would refuse. She might be foolish to forgo a chance to see more of Australia, when she was here, but after leaving Taronda, the farther she was away from Sloan Maddison the better. Back in England, she could hope to forget him. At least she would have some chance of building a new life. A London job and an apartment would probably be the answer. Looking down, noticing the wild country over which they were flying, Stacy wondered why no other place seemed to appeal much any more. There was only one place she wanted to be, and that was here with Sloan on Taronda.

Just over an hour and they were coming down at another Outback station which, from the air, was not unlike Taronda. On the airstrip where they landed were several small planes, but many guests, because Reeva was not so isolated as Taronda, had arrived by car. A variety of vehicles were parked all over the place, with people waving and greeting each other on all sides.

The party from Taronda was seen immediately, the owner of Reeva, Ben Sawyers, Jill's father, having come out himself to meet them—something of an honour, Paula whispered in Stacy's ear, among so many guests. But then Sloan was never overlooked. It touched Stacy immensely, Paula's obvious pride in the son she never quite managed to understand. Quite a crowd joined the group around him, and Stacy was aware, with a glow of unaccountable pleasure, of how he was constantly deferred to. If she hadn't known it before, she was left in no doubt that, in Queensland at any rate, Sloan Maddison was a man of some consequence.

The house at Reeva was not as big as the one at Taronda, but it was impressive, all the same, with its grounds brightly lit in the failing light and laughter and music echoing from both inside and out. People were dancing, others drinking and exchanging gossip, some were even swimming in the pool. There was such a whirl of noise and activity that Stacy's mind boggled to imagine this going on all night.

Like a lovely flame in her pale dress, she stayed by Paula while Bill and Sally danced. Sloan stood nearby, again talking to his host, who seemed bent on having Sloan's opinion. Occasionally Sloan glanced towards them, Stacy assumed to assure himself his mother was all right, and that she herself was behaving! He was so tall and handsome, with his dark head and lean, strong body. Despairingly Stacy thought he must be the best-looking man in the room.

Others apparently believed it too. She saw the naked admiration in Barbara Bolam's eyes as she approached, dragging behind her a slightly younger man who looked rather like her. Stacy was not surprised when Paula hissed, 'Barbara's brother!'

Immediately Barbara annexed Sloan, saying she was sorry she had just arrived, as though she hadn't been summing up the situation for the last five minutes. Stretching up, she coolly kissed Sloan's cheek, sliding her two hands around his arm and pressing tightly against him, giving him what Stacy supposed was meant to be tantalising glimpses of the gleaming white flesh that overflowed abundantly from a tight but beautifully fashioned black dress. Barbara looked the picture of radiant confidence, and how much more so would she be if she could have heard what Sloan had said about taking a wife.

Barbara, as soon as she thought it safe to turn her attention from Sloan for a minute, introduced Stacy to her brother. 'I promised Reg a surprise,' she said glibly, ignoring Sloan's frown.

Stacy, unfortunately, took an instant dislike to Reg Bolam. Somehow he reminded her of Basil Bradley, although he looked quite different. He asked her to dance, and while she couldn't very well refuse she could tell by the way he held her she wasn't going to improve on her first impression.

'Barbara's been telling me about you,' Reg grinned, holding her away from him, not from ordinary politeness, she realised, but so he could blatantly study every detail of her figure. When she tensed, he just laughed and pulled her closer. 'I like to look at what I like, if you see what I mean, darling? I don't always stick to looking, either.'

'Are you a—a cattleman, Mr Bolam?' she gasped, having no wish to make a scene, but having great difficulty in preventing herself from slapping his leering face. It was an impulse which had to be restrained, if she hoped to avoid Sloan's wrath, for naturally he wouldn't appreciate it if she insulted his bride-to-be's brother.

'A cattleman? Sure,' he laughed, 'and we own plenty! My current girl-friend considers she's on to a good thing, but she's not half as beautiful as you.'

Stacy felt sorry for her, but again she strove to be polite. She couldn't raise a smile, but she did try to be civil. 'Maybe I'm just a little different.'

'You're that all right!' He was surveying her too closely again, making Stacy aware she had merely managed to increase his interest, not allay it. 'No wonder Sloan has been keeping you out of sight. I can understand why Barbara's been getting worried.'

'I'm afraid I don't follow you.'

'You don't? Really, darling, I could have sworn you weren't dumb.'

'Mr Bolam!' she protested, disliking his silly, loaded remarks as much as she was beginning to dislike him. 'You shouldn't be talking to me like this. You seem to forget we're strangers. I don't know your sister well, either, as I've only met her once before, but I wouldn't do anything to hurt her. I happen to be aware that Sloan and she are good friends.'

'Ha!' he sneered cynically. 'That's one way of putting it!'

Stacy hated suggestive men and was glad to escape this

one, especially as his last sly insinuation made her go cold. When Sally and Bill rescued her at the end of that particular dance, she breathed a sigh of relief.

'Heavy going?' Sally whispered, as a small blonde girl physically inserted herself between Stacy and Reg.

'You might say.' Stacy kept her voice low but glanced at Sally gratefully.

'Don't worry, I'm sure I can find plenty of men you'll be glad to meet,' Sally teased softly, and with a quickly comprehensive look at Stacy's disturbed face, proceeded to do just that.

For a while Stacy almost enjoyed herself, as she danced with men, who might be admiring but were also conventional and decently friendly. Reg kept returning, though, in spite of her discreet endeavours to head him off, and she began to feel alarmed that it must appear to be becoming a kind of tug-of-war between herself and the little blonde girl.

Eventually Sloan asked her to dance. 'You look as if it's all getting too much for you,' he said grimly. 'How's the head?'

She could have told him Reg Bolam was bothering her more. 'Much better, thank you,' she replied, having a horrible suspicion it was going to begin aching in earnest any minute now.

He looked down on her, frowning. 'Sally and Bill arriving as they did rather took our attention from the fright you got when you were lost. You might have suffered more than I thought.'

'I don't think you need worry. I've recovered.' She turned her head up to him, her eyes unconsciously appealing. 'I've thought a lot about that poor kangaroo, though, and your truck.'

'Well, you can stop worrying about the truck,' he said drily. 'It's been rescued. As for the kangaroo, I doubt very much if it will be missed. They're a national pest, if the rest of the world would only believe it. They multiply too rapidly and do untold damage.'

'Just like rabbits can do at home.'

'We have our share of those, too, but they aren't as bad as the kangaroo.'

'I still don't feel too proud that I was responsible for the death of one of them.'

'Stacy!' He looked down at her, his eyes brushing intently over her soft mouth. 'Not even for you will I spend an entire dance discussing a kangaroo.'

Mutinously, she pulled away from him. 'Don't make it sound as if you consider me something special, like Barbara Bolam!'

'Another minute and I'll shake you!' He pulled her back, as though to punish her, so she seemed to feel every bit of him, as his arms tightened, down the whole length of her slim body. 'But as you've mentioned Barbara, I'd better advise you to stop encouraging her brother. You might be used to men like Reg Bolam, but facts seem to prove you can't manage them. You wouldn't want another Basil Bradley on your hands, now would you?'

CHAPTER TEN

STACY considered Sloan's words both uncalled-for and cruel, but as he was determined to think the worst of her it could be both a waste of time and nervous energy to argue with him. 'I think I can look after myself,' she tried to ignore the cynical twist to his mouth. 'Can't we talk—about something else?'

He swung her around abruptly, as though he would have liked to hurt her. 'What about? I noticed you didn't do much talking when you danced with Reg Bolam.'

Couldn't he leave it? After all, hadn't he been enjoying himself with other girls, particularly Barbara? Unable not to sound bitter, she commented, 'It doesn't look as if you're going to be too lonely when your mother goes.'

'I wasn't aware she'd come to any final decision.'

Her eyes full of unconscious reproach, Stacy looked at him. 'You know very well she'll choose to go with Sally. I imagine you had a hand in it, and I can't say I'm surprised.'

'I wonder, Stacy,' he held her gaze, his own entirely mocking, 'how you come to have so many lovers, when you're so suspicious of a man's motives?'

'You aren't my lover.' Why was there such a strange weakness in her limbs at the thought of it?

'I could be very easily, that is if I thought you were open to proposition.'

Swallowing hard, she lowered her head, trying desperately to emulate his mockery. 'I'll soon be gone. It would scarcely be worth the bother.'

'No,' he agreed tightly, 'it might not. Not when I'm considering something more permanent.'

Pain danced with her, with the knowledge that he was at

168

last marrying Barbara. He had made up his mind, and the sooner Stacy escaped from Taronda the better. The face she raised was white, but her voice was steady. 'I haven't asked your mother if she intends going to Brisbane with Sally and Bill, when they leave.'

'They'll only be staying another day or two.'

'Whatever your mother decides, I think I'll go back with them. I can get a plane from Brisbane and it will save you making a special journey.'

'I had no intention of taking you anywhere,' he said.

They danced in silence after that, Sloan's arms strangely rigid around Stacy's cold young body. Unhappiness numbed her as they danced slowly around the room. Not one single word of regret had left his lips about her going, and she felt suddenly shaken to the core by the depth of her own heartache.

Yet if Sloan's complete indifference to her departure seemed a disaster, it wasn't half as bad as the one which happened later.

After supper, because the sight of Sloan and Barbara dancing together was inescapable, Stacy slipped out to the gardens. Seeking the shadows, she allowed herself a private moment to indulge her misery. Just another few days, no longer, and she would be gone. All she could hope for was that she might manage this with dignity. No last-minute tears must be allowed to give Sloan a perverted satisfaction. Somehow she must prove she had no regrets about leaving him.

Stacy lingered under some trees, welcoming the dark protection of their branches. The moonlight was bright, and while she had never seen such brilliance, she didn't appreciate it tonight. She would rather have had total darkness to hide her misery, but at least she had this corner to herself. It was then that Reg Bolam found her, and his appearance filled her with fright.

'Ah, here you are!' His teeth flashed boldly, as if he was

surprised to find her here, as if he hadn't been monitoring her every movement closely since Barbara had introduced them.

The typical villain, Stacy thought wildly, a mildly hysterical desire to laugh sweeping over her as she backed away from him. Didn't her life seem full of them?

'I guessed you'd be pleased to see me.' His vanity matched his sister's, as he mistook the glitter in her eyes for pleasure. 'You getting some fresh air? I guess we have plenty of that!'

'Yes.' Fresh air was about all Stacy was prepared to discuss with him. 'It's nice and cool out here.'

'But you'd consider it an insult if it remained like that when I was around,' he smirked outrageously.

'Really, Mr Bolam,' she forced herself to stay calm, 'I'm sure your girl-friend is waiting, and I'm ready to go back now.'

'I'm not,' he said abruptly, his voice thickening as he stared down on her, his hands reaching out. 'You really take my fancy, darling.'

Oh, where, Stacy wondered frantically, as his hands closed over her shoulders, were all the nice men she had been dancing with? How was it she always attracted the worst types, and every country had its share—this she was learning, to her cost. 'Let me go!' she gasped. 'I'm afraid I don't fancy you, Mr Bolam.'

'Come on, come on,' his grip tightened, 'you can't expect me to let you go. And make it Reg, sweetheart. Sounds much more friendly.'

'Please, let me go!' She didn't bother to keep her voice down. 'Can't you take no for an answer!'

'Why should I?' Suddenly, without warning, he lowered his head and kissed her.

At first stunned, she couldn't move, then she began struggling wildly. 'Don't touch me!' she cried, wrenching her mouth from his, terrified of the glazed, animal-like look in his eyes, the determined, unleashed desire.

'I want to do more than that, darling!' He hauled her to him again while she sought fiercely to evade him.

This only served to incite him further. As Stacy jerked backwards, his hands missed her shoulders and caught the front of her dress, so that the fine material ripped as he tore at it savagely.

Horror lent Stacy the strength to make one last bid for freedom. With all her might she put her hands against his chest and pushed him away. His thick, hot breath almost suffocated her, but she kicked fiercely with her feet and twisted, until she was free. Instantly he was after her and, while she might have escaped, she tripped on her long skirts and they both tumbled to the ground.

There, in an instant, as she lay winded, Reg Bolam's mouth fastened ravenously on hers, and she was unable to fight him.

'Get up!'

Stacy didn't think she had ever heard Sloan's voice so blazingly full of anger. In her dazed state it came to her in waves, each one hitting her with excruciating force. Total relief came as Reg, cursing loudly, rolled away from her, but it disappeared immediately she opened stunned eyes to meet the vicious contempt in Sloan's. This time, she knew, she was condemned for ever.

As Reg rose slowly, but far from silently, to his feet, Sloan's fist shot out, contacting his chin so relentlessly that the crack was frightening. There was violence in the brutal way he smashed Reg to the ground. Stacy found herself kneeling, staring numbly at his prone body, in a kind of blind dismay. He lay so still she wondered if Sloan had killed him. She heard Barbara scream, in the same moment as Sloan took hold of her and hauled her to her feet.

Barbara spoke shrilly, as she took Stacy's place by her brother's side. 'It wasn't Reg's fault, Sloan, anyone could see. You had no reason to hit him. That girl was leading him on!'

Sloan didn't answer her, he was too busy looking at

Stacy. Even in the moonlight it wasn't difficult to see her dress was torn, although the wind, blowing it about her, disguised the worst of the damage, hiding much of her bared flesh. Silently, his mouth a tight line, he removed his jacket and draped it around her shaking shoulders. 'I'll take you home,' he said, so coldly it nearly turned Stacy's blood to ice.

She didn't know what to say, never having felt so helplessly unnerved in her life. She had no wish to stay here any longer. If people found out what had happened she didn't think she could bear it, yet if Sloan took her home would it not cause even more conjecture? While she hesitated, the matter was taken out of her hands when she was physically sick. She had just time to stumble away from Sloan before it overcame her, but he caught up, holding her firmly until the worst had passed, and she was able to say weakly, 'I could wait in the plane until the party is over. I don't want to spoil your fun.'

'God help me!' she heard Sloan exclaim, half under his breath. 'Another word from you and I'll let that imbecile over there have you. Do you intend providing a free show for everybody? There'll be enough talk as it is.'

'Whatever you like,' she whispered hoarsely, shock beginning to take effect so she didn't care any more. It didn't seem important that Sloan was staring at her as though he hated the sight of her. Trying to walk away from him, she felt her legs buckle, and the last thing she was aware of was Sloan's arms catching her as she fell against him, unconscious.

They were back at Taronda before she came round. Sloan must have strapped her in, as he was unloosening the safety harness and lifting her from the plane.

As she opened her mouth to protest, he said grimly, 'We're home now, so don't make any more fuss about leaving Reeva.'

'Home?' she repeated, tears streaming unchecked at the word. What wouldn't she give for the right to call Taronda home? 'I was only going to say I can walk,' she sobbed, as he carried her towards the waiting truck.

'I would only have to go to the trouble of picking you up again,' he snapped, 'so dry your tears; they don't impress me, I'm afraid.'

In the truck, for all her attempts to sit straight, she kept tumbling against him, and as his hand constantly steadied her she felt her head swim, and more sobs rise to her throat.

'If you don't stop it,' he said savagely, 'I'll hit you, harder than I hit Reg.'

She couldn't believe he would, but the sharpness of his voice, the threat behind his words, strengthened her. 'I hate you!' she cried.

'Good,' he returned curtly. 'I like my feelings reciprocated exactly!'

Driving straight to the front of the house, he appeared to have little compunction about wakening everyody. Fortunately this didn't happen. Taronda slept on, unaware that its tall owner was carrying a shivering girl half naked to her bedroom, his face like granite.

Once there he flung her on her bed, oblivious of her painful murmur. Stacy saw he was still in his shirt sleeves and that his shirt was filthy, covered with dust and bits of grass from her head. It was then she realised her forehead was sore, where she had hit it as she had fallen, on the dusty earth under the trees. When she put tentative fingers to it, they came away covered with dirt and something else.

Sloan didn't notice. He looked down at his shirt with distaste, then wrenched it off, before coming down beside her on the bed. Not touching her, he stared at her, his face grim. 'You little slut!' he snarled, 'you've actually been rolling in the dust; your face is covered with it. Is this some new form of sex I haven't heard of?'

'Please!' Her face stark white, her eyes tormented, she begged him, 'You don't understand, and you wouldn't believe me.'

'Too true.' He took no notice of her tearful entreaty. 'I'd

better have my jacket, then I'll leave you to get cleaned up, while I get back to Reeva and collect the others. I'll get you a drink before I go.'

'Thank you for helping me.' She made a great effort to pull herself together, to speak coolly. 'I can manage now. I'll have a bath, as soon as you're away.' Terrified of breaking down again, she began stripping off his jacket, struggling out of it, not aware how her torn dress left her almost naked to the waist. It was only as she saw Sloan's eyes fixed on her, his face flushing a dark red, that she glanced down at herself and understood.

His mouth tightened into angry lines, his face was grim as he took the jacket and flung it aside, so he could better see her bruised shoulders.

'I'm sorry about your jacket and shirt.' Stacy tried to find something to cover herself, in the middle of her abject apology, but when he wrenched the sheet from her fingers and she met the dark fury in his eyes, the rush of tears to her own eyes made her lips tremble.

'Leave it,' he commanded, coming down beside her again, his fingers fastening on her chin to turn her face up to his. His hand tightened, as if he had a fancy to strangle her. 'It seems that Reg was with you longer than I thought.'

'You're hurting me, Sloan,' she gasped, unable to face the fire in his glance as he deliberately let it roam her bare body. 'Please . . .' The rest of her sentence was lost as his mouth came down on hers and he pressed her back against the pillows, his hands holding her shoulders perfectly still until he felt the fight go out of her. Then, as his probing mouth parted her lips, his hands slid to her breast, caressing the sensitive fullness he found there.

She shivered, reacting deeply to the touch of his hands, the crushing pressure of his mouth following them, taking and giving, threatening yet promising ecstasy. The ultimate, after the first traumatic step, if she were brave enough to give him what he seemed to be asking for.

His mouth probed hungrily against the upthrust of her breasts and she groaned. 'I could kill you,' he said unsteadily, 'Did he make love to you?'

'No.' Knowing what he meant, she fought to deny it.

'Do you want me to believe you, Stacy?'

'Yes.' How could she concentrate on Reg with Sloan caressing her as he was?

He lifted his head reluctantly, his breathing fast. 'Once you said you loved me, Stacy. Did you mean it?'

She moved restlessly, feeling her heartbeat quicken and trying to hide it from him. Seeing the doubt on his face, the way his eyes narrowed, made denial easier. 'I'm not sure,' she faltered.

'Aren't you?' His eyes flamed as his arms slipped around her back, crushing her to him. Holding her pressed closely against the roughness of his bare chest, his hand moved to the throat, fingering the white skin before forcing her mouth up to meet his, bringing her to such a pitch of desire that she moaned again.

Her hands lifted, she couldn't stop them moving over him, searching his powerful chest, his wide, smooth shoulders until he shuddered. Her slender body melted against him and she felt the desire in him shaping her to him as her urgent fingers slid upwards into his thick hair.

'Say it now,' he whispered thickly, his eyes glittering on her flushed face, her warm, trembling mouth with a curious hardness.

'I love you,' she gasped, her heart running wild, helpless in the grip of such sensual excitement which was increasing to a white-hot heat between them.

He breathed fast, his look a challenge. 'What if I asked you to prove you'd never belonged to another man?'

Stacy was beyond thought, no other desire in her head but to submit to him. She couldn't concentrate on how she might convince him. 'You have my word,' she said helplessly, her lips pressing feverishly against the firmness of

his cheek, as he kept his mouth just tantalisingly out of
reach.

'It's not enough, Stacy.'

'No ...' She didn't need him to tell her, but her aware-
ness was coming more from the senses than rational
thought. She could feel the deep need in him and it made
her tremble, deep down in every hidden nerve of her slender body.

'I have to have you, Stacy, you know that, one way or
another.' His eyes fastened on the moist parting of her lips
and he seemed to take her surrender for granted as he eased
his long length on to the bed beside her.

As she felt the strong muscles of his thighs moving intently against the melting fire in her limbs, hot tears made
Stacy's eyes ache, and she knew she could go on resisting
him no more than she could her own passionate nature. This
Sloan was revealing to her so mercilessly that she felt she
was being battered and swept by a storm against which she
had no defence. Bemused, she hung back, but he caught
her lips, swiftly taking possession of them with a hunger
that sent wild flames of desire driving through her until she
was clinging to him mindlessly. No more words were spoken,
but her consent seemed given in the urgent clinging of her
arms, the intoxicating, sensual sweetness which was forcing
every inch of her towards ultimate surrender.

The fierce hunger in him rocked and frightened her at
first, but gradually his breathing changed. He lay beside
her until the pulsing hardness of his body had her fully
aroused, and his mouth lifted slowly from hers as she
waited.

'You're very sure?' His voice was low as he paused, as
his hand came up gently to lift the heavy hair from off her
hot forehead. It was then, as he seemed to see for the first
time the full extent of the severe bruising which her hair had
partly hidden, that he halted abruptly, the blaze of passion
on his face slowly subsiding.

For a long moment he didn't speak, as his strong features went stony hard. With soft violence in his voice, he asked, 'Who did this, Stacy?' His fingers probed gently. 'Was it Bolam?'

'No!' The wound was throbbing, but so was her heart. One she could endure, the other was making her feel so restless she couldn't stand it! 'It doesn't matter, Sloan.'

'Of course it does!' To examine the dust-covered cuts more closely, he pushed every strand of hair from off her brow. Savagely he asked, 'If Bolam didn't do it, how did it happen?'

'Happen?' Stacey's clouded gaze lacked concentration. Sloan's image was blurred, but she found it difficult to take her eyes off him, to take her mind from his lovemaking. 'It was when I was trying to get away from him.'

Clipped were Sloan's tones, as if he wasn't finding it too easy to adjust himself. 'I told you to behave yourself, not to encourage him.'

'I didn't, Sloan.' Her clear young voice sounded unconsciously hurt that he should think she had. 'He found me in the garden.'

'Why were you there by yourself?'

The sudden harshness in him made her sigh, while her dazed state precluded everything but the truth. 'Maybe I got tired of seeing you dancing with Miss Bolam.' This reminded Stacy that although Sloan had made her confess her love for him, he had never breathed a word about his own feelings. When his love was so obviously reserved for Barbara, why did he wonder that Stacy had sought to escape from the sight of them dancing together? 'I certainly never encouraged Reg Bolam. I don't even like him and I doubt if he really likes me. All he likes is his own way!'

'So what did happen?'

Stacy put up her hands to pull his away from her head, but she didn't succeed. Sloan merely muttered, 'Stop it,' as he kept them there, waiting for her answer.

Quivering with reluctance, she whispered, 'He must have followed, and then he wanted to make love to me. I told him I wasn't interested and when he wouldn't listen I managed to push him away. That was when I tripped over my long skirt and we both fell.'

'That was all?'

'Wasn't it enough?' she asked bitterly.

'I'll probably break every bone of his body,' Sloan said calmly, only a certain whiteness under his skin hinting at the anger raging through him. 'No one treats—a guest of mine this way.'

Clearly, Stacy understood. Anyone staying at Taronda must be treated with consideration. Sloan would consider her accident in this light, and it would be solely from this point of view he would seek vengeance. 'It doesn't matter,' she insisted, wondering if anything ever would now.

Slowly Sloan stood up and passed her her bathrobe. 'Put that on,' he said flatly, 'and we'll go and get that head washed.'

'Thank you,' she managed to say, her head throbbing painfully again, her hands suddenly shaking. The grimness of his face made her tremble so much she could do nothing with the robe but stare at it helplessly, tears running down her grubby cheeks again. 'I'm sorry,' she stammered, looking away from him.

He seemed so angry at her weakness that she shrank, remembering her nakedness, her face hot. But there was no embarrassment about him as he helped her into her robe, although his jaw was rigid. Then, as if knowing the exact state of her limbs without having to be told, he picked her up and carried her through to the bathroom, her slight weight cradled carefully against him.

'What about your mother and Sally?' she reminded him feebly.

He put her down gently and her robe fell apart. 'That was before,' he said, rather indistinctly, fastening her sash, his hands pushing against her slim midriff, sending fresh shivers through her.

'Now,' he said harshly, turning from her to run the hot tap, 'stop worrying about other people while I get your head seen to.' His hands were so gentle as he bathed her face, she almost didn't notice the stinging pain. The water was exactly the right heat and he laced it with antiseptic, but his eyes hardened grimly as he saw the depth of some of the grazing. 'However did you manage it?' he raged.

'I seemed to skid along the ground, where it was bare and stony under some trees,' she explained, beginning to feel curiously exhausted for all she was letting Sloan do all the work.

'It's a wonder you weren't knocked out,' he said tersely, removing the last dampness from her cheeks before taking her back to the bedroom. When she was safely on her bed again, he said, 'Be getting in while I fetch you something to drink. If you can't do with one, I can.'

A few minutes later he returned. 'Get that down you.' He passed her a glass, seeing that while she had managed to put on her nightdress and climb into bed, she was still far too pale.

'I think it would make me sick.' Tearfully she stared at the golden-brown liquid.

'Stacy!'

Quickly, wanting to appease him, she took a quick sip, surprised to find it did make her feel better. She noticed, with a warm flush, that he had found a clean shirt which he tucked in his trousers as he had his own drink.

The brandy made her feel sleepy and she made no protest when Sloan dropped beside her, although she quickly averted her eyes. The sight of his long, hard body still had the power to make hers ache. He was so near, yet he sat away from her and she felt lonely, filled with a painful longing which not even the soreness of her head could dissipate. Desolately, she had to ask, 'Are you going now?'

'No, Stacy.' His eyes burned, but he kept his voice even, so as not to frighten her. 'I'm not leaving you until you're asleep and Mrs Turner is here to take over.'

'But your mother?'

'Stacy, for God's sake relax!' He continued to watch her face, noting her blue eyes filling with tears, her mouth quivering with nerves and misery. 'Just go to sleep, you'll feel better when you wake up. Someone will bring them back; quite frankly I wouldn't care if they never got here.'

What did he mean? Obediently she closed her eyes, feeling a sudden compulsion to obey him in all things. 'You seem to be forever rescuing me,' she whispered, the brandy beginning to take effect as tiredness washed over her.

His hands, amazingly adept but briefly unsteady, tucked her in, willing her to lie still, but she tossed restlessly, clutching at him as he bent over her. 'Please hold me, Sloan,' she begged feverishly. 'I don't want to be alone.'

A muscle jerked at the side of his mouth as he stared down at her; she heard the breath drag in his throat, as if she was asking the impossible, and she felt an incredible sense of relief when he did as she asked.

'You aren't alone,' he sighed deeply, as he pulled her close, as he sank down by her again, his hands going soothingly over her bright head. 'Oh, Stacy, go to sleep. It will soon be dawn,' he said, the heat of his body already warming and comforting her.

That was the last thing she remembered until she woke up.

It didn't seem possible, in view of Sloan's concern, that next morning he should be so changed. It was after ten when she woke, her head still bruised and slightly sore, but otherwise she didn't feel any the worse. The room was warm, but she shivered as she recalled everything that had happened, but as Sloan had promised, she did feel better this morning than she had thought she would.

Putting a curious hand to her head, she slid out of bed,

her satiny nightgown clinging to her soft curves as she crossed the room to look in the mirror. Her brow did seem a bit of a mess, but she guessed the scratches were mostly superficial and would soon heal. Colour crept into the paleness of her cheeks as she thought of Sloan, but receded as the image of Barbara Bolam intruded. There was a thrill of excitement on remembering his kisses, then the darkness of despondency as she realised he didn't love her, that his kindness and help would have been given to anyone in need of it.

Finding a cool cotton skirt, she was dressed, ready to go downstairs when Mrs Turner came in with a tray, fussing because she was out of bed, saying Sloan would flay her alive if Stacy came to any harm. If Sloan's apparent concern was comforting, Stacy also found it puzzling, especially when she learned he had gone out for the day. Mrs Maddison, with Sally and Bill, had only got home an hour ago, and, after assuring themselves that Stacy was recovering, had gone to rest. Mrs Turner, after parting with this information, said Sloan expected to be back in time for dinner.

It seemed that everyone understood that Stacy had lost her way in the gardens at Reeva, and bumped into a tree, and to save disrupting the party, Sloan had brought her straight home. Gathering for pre-dinner drinks with her family that evening, Paula decided Stacy, with a fine bandage over her brow and tied at the back of her head, looked really too vividly attractive to have much the matter with her. The effect of pure white against her pale skin and abundance of bright hair was stunningly eye-catching, and to hear Sloan on the subject of last night, one would have thought the girl at death's door. When he had got in touch he had sounded so terse, she had worried throughout the remainder of the party.

When Sloan joined them, however, he merely asked Stacy politely if she felt better, then scarcely spoke to her at all, which left Paula more confused than ever.

After dinner, when Paula announced that she had something to tell them, Stacy wasn't very surprised. As she rose to leave them, Paula asked her to stay as, unfortunately, what she had to say concerned Stacy as well. She said she had decided to go to Brisbane and live near Sally, so she wouldn't be going to Bilton Manor after all. Looking slightly ashamed, she promised Stacy she would speak to her privately next morning.

This she did, promising Stacy she wouldn't lose out. She would be compensated with a year's salary and all her expenses paid. Paula assured her she could quite afford it and Sloan had agreed.

Stacy refused, though without any resentment, feeling Paula had been generous enough already. She was too aware that no money could lessen the pain of her impending parting from Sloan. Thorn Farm and England, or Bilton Manor, were not important any more. During the following two days, as she was waiting numbly to leave with Paula and the others for Brisbane, she discovered that her love for Sloan was greater than that which she had for any place on earth. With Sloan she could have been happy anywhere, without him her life might not be worth living.

Sloan, on the much discussed subject of Paula's departure, had little to say other than to give his approval. Apart from dinner, after which he usually disappeared into his study, they saw little of him. Knowing he must be secretly embarrassed by the way she had clung to him after he had brought her back from the party, Stacy made no attempt to seek him out. Instead she continued to play with the children and went riding with Sally and Bill. Other times she talked with Paula and helped Mrs Turner, while her heart hungered, unfulfilled and strain made her look pale and ill.

On the night before they were due to fly out she was wandering tearfully in the garden in the darkness when

Sloan found her. Startled to see him, she tried to wipe away her tears before he saw them. Throughout dinner he had looked so grim, even Sally had been wary.

'All packed?' He stopped a few feet away, arrogant in his stance, his keen gaze penetrating the darkness.

'Yes.' It was all Stacy could find to say, and she was glad the shadows hid her trembling.

'Then you've been wasting your time, I'm afraid. You aren't going anywhere.'

His words were ambiguous, but it was something in his voice which made her falter, to stare up at him in anguish. 'I have to go, you know that.'

'Yes.' Now his voice held total mastery, compelling her to go along with him, only a slight harshness betraying that he might easily resort to violence if she dissented. 'But we'll leave together, after our wedding, on a honeymoon.'

'Sloan!' she cried, tangled in his choice of words, her eyes brilliant with shattered emotion. 'Stop teasing me, I can't stand it.'

'Teasing you!' With a muttered curse he stepped forward, catching her cruelly to him. 'Oh, Stacy,' he groaned against her neck, 'do you think I would? Don't you understand that I'm asking you to marry me? I refuse to let you put me through hell any longer. You can make up your mind you're going to do something about it, and soon!'

'You can't be serious?' She felt stunned, her heart racing under his hand until she felt faint.

'I've never been more serious in my life.' His eyes darkening, he considered her shaking lips through the darkness, his intention very clear. 'Did you really think I'd let you go?'

Pushing against his tightening arms, Stacy felt her head whirl. Her traitorous body demanded her instantaneous surrender, but her brain showed her another side of things. In desperation she fought to stay cool.

'Sloan, you've hated me since I came here—I suppose since you found out about Basil Bradley. I did begin to believe you were beginning to have second thoughts about him and learning to trust me, but these last two days you've never come near me.'

There was a strained silence as he pulled her back to him. She heard his breath rasp as his hand gripped her soft chin, turning her face up to him. 'If you must have a lengthy explanation, don't provoke me, Stacy, by trying to get away.' The touch of his hands sent hot flames leaping through her body, as did the hard kiss he dropped on her warm, but trembling mouth. 'I'm warning you,' he said thickly, 'I can't stand much more.'

'Do you love me, Sloan,' she was curiously distraught at his quick anger, 'or do you want to marry me for some other reason?'

'Because I love you.' His eyes were riveted on her reactions, as though he derived a tyrannical pleasure from her transparent inability to resist him. 'Yes, I love you,' he repeated hoarsely, the desire to hurt going out of him as his lips moved against her cheek. 'I fell in love with you in England. I'm not sure when a violent attraction turned to love. I knew we had something going, but I didn't know I was getting in so deep. Then, quite suddenly, I had to have you. I wanted to marry you, to be able to love you in every possible way.'

'Why didn't you tell me?' she asked huskily.

He caught a tear with his mouth and rubbed the dampness over her parted lips. 'Because I had to get you here, to let you see what you could be letting yourself in for. You wouldn't have been the first girl to have got cold feet at the sight of such wild isolation. I realise Taronda is comfortable, but the setting will never change, and my wife will be here for a lifetime because I won't ever let her go. Then, when fate, in the form of my mother's illness, seemed to be lending a kindly hand, I had to find out about Basil Bradley. That just about finished me!' he groaned.

'Yet you still let me come here?'

'Because I fancied if I had to learn to hate you, to regain my peace of mind, it would be the quickest way. At the same time I was determined to find some way of punishing you, too. I might have known it wouldn't work when that month I waited was the longest I'd ever spent.'

'It was for me, too,' she breathed unevenly.

'Perhaps that doesn't surprise me.' He didn't try to hide a mocking masculinity, his mouth assaulting hers again. 'I soon learnt how your body responded to mine in every way, even when your mind objected.'

Colour came to her cheeks, and she knew his hand deliberately tested the heat of her skin, as he touched it.

Thickly, he said, 'I found out just how impossible it was to hate you that day you took the truck and got lost. That day, when I realised I might have lost you for ever, I suddenly knew what a fool I'd been. From that moment, Stacy, I believed absolutely in your innocence. I know that later I asked you to prove it, but you had me beyond rational thought. I was willing to grasp at anything for an excuse.'

'Oh, Sloan!' she whispered, colour running wildly through her already flushed cheeks.

His eyes glittered with remorse as he stared down at her. 'You'll never know how much I regretted listening to that woman in Birmingham. Or for ever doubting you in the first place.'

Her eyes held his, tender with love. 'It doesn't matter now, darling, but I only wish you'd told me sooner. I thought you loved Barbara Bolam.'

'No,' he shook his head ruefully. 'That day in Cairns, we'd just bumped into each other an hour before, and she insisted on coming to the airport. I haven't led a particularly monkish life, Stacy, but she and I have never been lovers. I used her a little to make you jealous, but that was all, and after what I said to her heel of a brother I doubt if we'll be seeing either of them again. I could have killed him that night, and enjoyed doing it. As for telling you I loved you sooner,' his voice deepened savagely, 'don't you think I wanted to? Not only had I judged you wrongly, I'd had no right to judge you at all. I love the innocence you bring to me, Stacy, but if you'd had a dozen lovers I would still want to love and cherish you.'

'I thought you wanted me to go,' she said tearfully.

'Never that,' he said fiercely. 'It was this terrible conviction I had that you must have these last two days to come to a definite decision. I've gone through hell, Stacy, and your face at dinner tonight convinced me you had, too. I had a feeling we were both wasting valuable time. At least I hope I was right.'

'I think I was slowly dying,' she moaned, as his hands went over her. 'It was like being tortured to death, I love you so much.'

'If it takes the rest of our lives, I'll make it up to you.' Deep passion roughened his voice as he spoke, but his mouth softened, as if the prospect was not too daunting. 'We'll get the wedding over, then I can begin.'

She smiled, a small, feline creature, not yet aware of her full power, as she wrapped her arms around him, feeling the urgent tightening of his limbs against her own. 'Won't we be married in England?' she queried uncertainly.

'No!' He pulled her closer to him, arousing a passion he dared her deny. 'We can go there afterwards, to see your mother and June. I love you and trust you, but I'm not allowing you out of my sight until we're married, and that's going to be right here.'

The night wind encircled them as they clung together for wordless moments, seeming to promise Stacy a happiness as endless and wild. Her face reflected the radiance within her, as Sloan turned her, with a regretful sigh, towards the house.

His arms stayed around her, his face softened into tender lines. 'We'd better go and put the others out of their misery. I believe Sally had her suspicions at dinner as to what was what was about to happen, and her curiosity must be killing her. Then I'll ring the preacher, just to make sure he does get here tomorrow.'

Stacy gasped. 'Weren't you taking an awfully high-handed risk?' she asked indignantly.

'Yes—well——' His eyes glinted, as he took total command. 'But it was worth it, don't you think?'

Sometimes, Stacy realised, with a tremulous sigh, as his arm tightened, there was nothing left for a girl to say but yes!

INTRODUCING

Harlequin Presents
Collection

An exciting new series
of early favorites from

Harlequin Presents

This is a golden opportunity
to discover these best-selling beautiful
love stories — available once again
for your reading enjoyment…

because Harlequin understands
how you feel about love.

Harlequin Presents
Collection

Available wherever Harlequin books are sold.

GREAT LOVE STORIES NEVER GROW OLD...

Like fine old Wedgwood, great love stories are timeless. The pleasure they bring does not decrease through the years. That's why Harlequin is proud to offer...

HARLEQUIN CLASSIC LIBRARY

Delightful old favorites from our early publishing program!

Each volume, first published more than 15 years ago, is an enchanting story of people in love. Each is beautifully bound in an exquisite Wedgwood-look cover. And all have the Harlequin magic, unchanged through the years!

Two **HARLEQUIN CLASSIC LIBRARY** volumes every month!
Available NOW wherever Harlequin books are sold.

SPECIAL

Harlequin Romance Treasury Book Offer

This superb Romance Treasury is yours at little or <u>no</u> cost.

3 exciting, full-length Romance novels in one beautiful hard-cover book.

**Introduce yourself to
Harlequin Romance Treasury.
The most beautiful books you've ever seen!**

Cover and spine of each volume features a distinctive gilt design.
An elegant bound-in ribbon bookmark completes the classic design.
No detail has been overlooked to make Romance Treasury
volumes as beautiful and lasting as the stories they contain.
What a delightful way to enjoy the very best and most popular
Harlequin romances again and again!

Here's how to get your volume NOW!

MAIL IN	$	GET
2 SPECIAL PROOF-OF-PURCHASE SEALS*	PLUS $1 U.S.	ONE BOOK
5 SPECIAL PROOF-OF-PURCHASE SEALS*	PLUS 50¢ U.S.	ONE BOOK
8 SPECIAL PROOF-OF-PURCHASE SEALS*	FREE	ONE BOOK

*Special proof-of-purchase seal from inside back cover of all specially marked Harlequin "Let Your Imagination Fly Sweepstakes" volumes. No other proof-of-purchase accepted.

ORDERING DETAILS:

Print your name, address, city, state or province, zip or postal code on the coupon below or a plain 3" x 5" piece of paper and together with the special proof-of-purchase seals and check or money order (no stamps or cash please) as indicated. Mail to:

HARLEQUIN ROMANCE TREASURY BOOK OFFER P.O. BOX 1399 MEDFORD, N.Y. 11763, U.S.A.

Make check or money order payable to: Harlequin Romance Treasury Offer. Allow 3 to 4 weeks for delivery.

Special offer expires: June 30, 1981.

PLEASE PRINT

Name

Address

Apt. No.

City

State/ Prov.

Zip/Postal Code

Let Your Imagination Fly Sweepstakes

Rules and Regulations:

NO PURCHASE NECESSARY

1. Enter the Let Your Imagination Fly Sweepstakes 1, 2 or 3 as often as you wish. Mail each entry form separately bearing sufficient postage. Specify the sweepstake you wish to enter on the outside of the envelope. Mail a completed entry form or, your name, address, and telephone number printed on a plain 3"x 5" piece of paper to:

HARLEQUIN LET YOUR IMAGINATION FLY
SWEEPSTAKES,
P.O. BOX 1280, MEDFORD, N.Y. 11763 U.S.A.

2. Each completed entry form must be accompanied by 1 Let Your Imagination Fly proof-of-purchase seal from the back inside cover of specially marked Let Your Imagination Fly Harlequin books (or the words "Let Your Imagination Fly" printed on a plain 3" x 5" piece of paper. Specify by number the Sweepstakes you are entering on the outside of the envelope.

3. The prize structure for each sweepstake is as follows:

Sweepstake 1 - North America

Grand Prize winner's choice: a one-week trip for two to either Bermuda; Montreal, Canada; or San Francisco. 3 Grand Prizes will be awarded (min. approx. retail value $1,375. U.S., based on Chicago departure) and 4,000 First Prizes: scarves by nik nik, worth $14. U.S. each. All prizes will be awarded.

Sweepstake 2 - Caribbean

Grand Prize winner's choice: a one-week trip for two to either Nassau, Bahamas; San Juan, Puerto Rico; or St. Thomas, Virgin Islands. 3 Grand Prizes will be awarded. (Min. approx. retail value $1,650. U.S., based on Chicago departure) and 4,000 First Prizes: simulated diamond pendants by Kenneth Jay Lane, worth $15. U.S. each. All prizes will be awarded.

Sweepstake 3 - Europe

Grand Prize winner's choice: a one-week trip for two to either London, England; Frankfurt, Germany; Paris, France; or Rome, Italy. 3 Grand Prizes will be awarded. (Min. approx. retail value $2,800. U.S., based on Chicago departure) and 4,000 First Prizes: 1/2 oz. bottles of perfume, BLAZER by Anne Klein. (Retail value over $30. U.S.). All prizes will be awarded.

Grand trip prizes will include coach round-trip airfare for two persons from the nearest commercial airport serviced by Delta Air Lines to the city as designated in the prize, double occupancy accommodation at a first-class or medium hotel, depending on vacation, and $500. U.S. spending money. Departure taxes, visas, passports; ground transportation to and from airports will be the responsibility of the winners.

4. To be eligible, Sweepstakes entries must be received as follows:
Sweepstake 1 Entries received by February 28, 1981
Sweepstake 2 Entries received by April 30, 1981
Sweepstake 3 Entries received by June 30, 1981
Make sure you enter each Sweepstake separately since entries will not be carried forward from one Sweepstake to the next.

The odds of winning will be determined by the number of entries received in each of the three sweepstakes. Canadian residents, in order to win any prize, will be required to first correctly answer a time-limited skill-testing question, to be posed by telephone, at a mutually convenient time.

5. Random selections to determine Sweepstake 1, 2 or 3 winners will be conducted by Lee Krost Associates, an independent judging organization whose decisions are final. Only one prize per family, per sweepstake. Prizes are non-transferable and non-refundable and no substitutions will be allowed. Winners will be responsible for any applicable federal, state and local taxes. Trips must be taken during normal tour periods before June 30, 1982. Reservations will be on a space-available basis. Airline tickets are non-transferable, non-refundable and non-redeemable for cash.

6. The Let Your Imagination Fly Sweepstakes is open to all residents of the United States of America and Canada, (excluding the Province of Quebec) except employees and their immediate families of Harlequin Enterprises Ltd., its advertising agencies, Marketing & Promotion Group Canada Ltd. and Lee Krost Associates, Inc., the independent judging company. Winners may be required to furnish proof of eligibility. Void wherever prohibited or restricted by law. All federal, state, provincial and local laws apply.

7. For a list of trip winners, send a stamped, self-addressed envelope to:
Harlequin Trip Winners List, P.O. Box 1401, MEDFORD, N.Y. 11763 U.S.A.
Winners lists will be available after the last sweepstake has been conducted and winners determined.
NO PURCHASE NECESSARY.

Let Your Imagination Fly Sweepstakes

OFFICIAL ENTRY FORM

Please enter me in Sweepstake No. _____

Please print:

Name _____

Address _____

Apt. No. _____ City _____

State/ _____ Zip/Postal
Prov. _____ Code _____

Telephone No. area code
( )

MAIL TO:
HARLEQUIN LET YOUR
IMAGINATION FLY SWEEPSTAKE No. _____
P.O. BOX 1280,
MEDFORD, N.Y. 11763 U.S.A.

(Please specify by number, the Sweepstakes you are entering.)

☐ **YES!**

Sign me up for the Historical Romance Book Club and send my FREE BOOKS! If I choose to stay in the club, I will pay only $8.50* each month, a savings of $6.48!

NAME: _____

ADDRESS: _____

TELEPHONE: _____

EMAIL: _____

☐ I want to pay by credit card.

☐ **VISA**   ☐ **MasterCard.**   ☐ **DISCOVER**

ACCOUNT #: _____

EXPIRATION DATE: _____

SIGNATURE: _____

Mail this page along with $2.00 shipping and handling to:
Historical Romance Book Club
PO Box 6640
Wayne, PA 19087
Or fax (must include credit card information) to:
610-995-9274
You can also sign up online at **www.dorchesterpub.com**.
*Plus $2.00 for shipping. Offer open to residents of the U.S. and Canada only. Canadian residents please call 1-800-481-9191 for pricing information.
If under 18, a parent or guardian must sign. Terms, prices and conditions subject to change. Subscription subject to acceptance. Dorchester Publishing reserves the right to reject any order or cancel any subscription.